# Praise

Waiting for Gabe is a story of the great unraveling done by grief, how it accrues in the body and ripples outwards to all it touches. But it is also a story of how hope can find us in the most impossible of ways. Stitching together life and afterlife, Black takes readers on an emotional journey both moving and unforgettable.

—**David Valdes**, author of *Spin Me Right Round*

# WAITING for GABE

*A Novel*

DIANA BLACK

LUCID HOUSE
PUBLISHING

# LU☾ID
# HOUSE
## PUBLISHING

Published in Marietta, Georgia, United States of America by Lucid House Publishing, LLC www.LucidHousePublishing.com.
©2024 by Diana Black
All rights reserved. First Edition.
This title is available in print and e-book.
Cover design and interior layout: The Design Lab/Jan Sharrow
Author photo: Kevin Garrett

This novel and its characters were created in the author's imagination over a period of years. Any resemblance to anyone living or dead is purely coincidental. If you or someone you love are suffering from suicidal thoughts, please seek professional help.

No part of this publication may be reproduced, stored, or introduced into a retrieval system or transmitted, in any form or by any means (electronic, mechanical, photocopying, recording, or otherwise) without the prior written permission of both the copyright owners and the publisher. The scanning, uploading, and distribution of this book via the internet or via any other means without the publisher's permission is illegal, and punishable by law. Please purchase only authorized print, electronic, or audio editions, and do not participate in or encourage electronic piracy of copyrightable materials. Brief quotations or excerpts in reviews of the book are the exception. Your support of the author's rights is appreciated.

Library of Congress Cataloging-in-Publication Data:
Black, Diana 1948-
Waiting for Gabe: a novel/ by Diana Black–1st ed.
Library of Congress Control Number: TK
Print ISBN: 9781950495566
E-book ISBN: 9781950495641

1. Loss of a child 2. Widower 3. Suicidal thoughts 4. Foster care 5. Organ donation 6. Grief 7. Ghosts 8. Romance 9. Christian 10. Unconditional love 11. Forgiveness

FIC0310170
FAM014000
FIC0420120

**Dedication**

To Jennifer and Caitlin
*"Hope is the thing with feathers."*
*— Emily Dickinson*

# Contents

| | |
|---|---|
| One: Gabe – Knockin' on Heaven's Door | 1 |
| Two: Gabe – The Big Dipper | 9 |
| Three: Gabe – Splash and Dash | 15 |
| Four: Irish – Earth Bound | 27 |
| Five: Cooder – A Falling Star | 37 |
| Six: Gabe – Angle of the Sun | 41 |
| Seven: Cooder – Quarter-Moon Dimples | 49 |
| Eight: Irish – What an Angel Wants | 53 |
| Nine: Gabe – It Must Be Destiny | 57 |
| Ten: Irish – The Plan | 67 |
| Eleven: Gabe – Choices | 75 |
| Twelve: Cooder – The First Visit | 81 |
| Thirteen: Irish – The First Visit | 87 |
| Fourteen: Gabe – Yellow Butterfly Pajamas | 93 |
| Fifteen: Jon – When Innocence Ruled | 101 |
| Sixteen: Cooder – Doc du Jour | 111 |
| Seventeen: Gabe – Up to the Task | 119 |
| Eighteen: Evan – Windows to the Soul | 123 |
| Nineteen: Irish – Pinstriped Broadcloth | 131 |
| Twenty: Gabe – The Plan | 135 |
| Twenty-One: Irish – The News | 141 |
| Twenty-Two: Cooder – Mockingbirds | 143 |
| Twenty-Three: Gabe – Obsessed | 151 |
| Twenty-Four: Mrs. Hisey – Walnut Street | 155 |
| Twenty-Five: Cooder – A Gut Memory | 161 |
| Twenty-Six: Irish – True Regret | 163 |

| | |
|---|---|
| Twenty-Seven: Gabe – The Vet Visit | 165 |
| Twenty-Eight: Michael – We Have a Problem | 167 |
| Twenty-Nine: Gabe – Mommy Tummy Worm | 175 |
| Thirty: Michael – The Huddle | 181 |
| Thirty-One: Gabe – A Brief Blessing | 185 |
| Thirty-Two: Gabe – Twice in One Day | 189 |
| Thirty-Three: Jon – They Steal Your Heart Away | 193 |
| Thirty-Four: The Guard – Window Four | 197 |
| Thirty-Five: Jon – The Badge | 199 |
| Thirty-Six: Gabe – Tall Weeds Wet with Dew | 203 |
| Thirty-Seven: Gabe – Something Left to Lose | 213 |
| Thirty-Eight: Gabe – The Barn Owl | 215 |
| Thirty-Nine: Gabe – Rest in Peace | 221 |
| Forty: Gabe – Waiting for Gabe | 225 |
| Epilogue | 231 |
| *Waiting for Gabe* by Diana Black: Book Club Questions | 236 |
| Acknowledgements | 238 |
| About the Author | 239 |

# ONE

## GABE – Knockin' on Heaven's Door

For the life of him, he can't remember what became of her birthday bike. "We're sorry for your loss," a Piney Valley officer had said when they seized the little Huffy as evidence. That he remembers like it was yesterday. Not to mention cocking his arm to throw a punch at the officer when someone, pretty sure he remembers who, stepped in and, thank God, grabbed his fist.

Of course, the officer was just doing his job. Police seized the bike to run a match on the car's blue paint found on the twisted pink bike frame. Thing is, what happened to the little Huffy once they had a paint match? Was the birthday bike with the big yellow bow pitched into a dark, dingy storage cage along with criminal evidence like chainsaws, switchblades, and shotguns?

Gabe adjusts the bed pillow to support the back of his head. For three years he hasn't thought twice about her bike, and now suddenly he's obsessed. And for all he can remember, the little Huffy could be out back in the utility garage.

◉ ◉ ◉

The utility garage. Gabriel George Hart bolts out of bed like a corpse come to life on a morgue slab.

He rummages in the dark for jeans and a flannel shirt, pulls on both, and barrels down the stairs two steps at a time.

For God's sakes, he's had a year. His bare feet pause on the bottom stair tread. Yeah, and he has until five o'clock that afternoon. Fourteen hours and counting. He studies the stairs leading back to the bedroom. Toss and turn obsessing about Leesie's birthday bike? Or write the blasted note?

In the dim light of the 40-watt bulb above the kitchen sink, Gabe tears open a phone bill stamped Final Notice. Using a nub of a pencil he's grabbed off the counter, he scribbles a few words on the blank side of the statement. He seals his note in the payment envelope and prints on the front TO WHOM IT MAY CONCERN. Immediately he regrets the unintended sarcasm. The hardened pencil eraser leaves a huge, ugly smudge, so he abandons his corrective efforts and tucks the envelope in his back jeans pocket.

Gabe scoops up his mud-caked boots from the spread of soiled newspapers on the kitchen floor and eases open the backdoor. God help him if Destiny awakens. The golden retriever will bolt outside and anoint every bush and tree in the backyard at least once.

The night is cold. His back braced against a porch post, he shivers and struggles to tug on his boots. Socks might have been a good idea and a jacket.

Pausing on the top porch step, rubbing his upper arms for warmth, he realizes Irish and Leesie were right. Stars blanketing Piney Valley are breathtaking. Just might miss them. "Nope," he mutters, pulling the envelope from his pocket and tapping it against his thigh. "Not going there." Words barely out of his mouth, he spots a meteor streaking across the sky like it's punctuating his comment with a long dash.

Irish would have loved that. She'd have gasped, "It's a sign!" But he isn't Irish.

Gabe is moved, however, by the sight of ice-dusted blades of grass overgrowing the steppingstones to the utility garage. If Leesie had seen them glistening in the moonlight, she'd have giggled, "Look, Daddy, the grass is frosted flaked!" The wisp of a memory from what seems like a lifetime ago makes him smile.

The white converted 15-passenger van with four flat tires abandoned in the utility garage stubbornly resists Gabe's best efforts to open its front passenger door. Determined, Gabe marches around the van and challenges the Econoline's driver door with extra muscle in his pull. Not a budge. Right, the trick is to lift up on the handle and push. When the door finally yields, Gabe's hit with the combined aroma of sour grass and sweat-soaked upholstery. Aah, he thinks, a smell only a hot air balloonist can love. He brushes a layer of dust off the van seat, coughs, then places the sealed envelope inside the glove box.

The van's interior light above his head flickers. *Irish, I'll give you that one. That is a sign.*

Gabe pops open the van hood and finds a repurposed plastic milk carton containing water. He smells the water inside and tops off the van's battery. He cleans and tightens ignition wires, checks the oil and plugs, tinkers here and tinkers there until nearly three hours later he finally eases closed the van hood.

With a rag from the work bench, he wipes his hands and visually inventories the garage. Discarded tires, paint cans, garden tools, and an old inflator fan. No sign of Leesie's little bike. He wonders how he'd have felt had he discovered the Huffy with the yellow bow among the clutter. God knows what he'd have done or how he'd have reacted. But he'd have liked the chance to find out.

Just shy of 6 a.m., Gabe emerges from the side door of the garage, rubs his lower back, and gazes at Fallow Ridge a mile to the east. Sunrise is a good half hour away. He darts toward the house where he pulls off his boots, drags himself upstairs to the bedroom, discards his flannel shirt and jeans on the hardwood floor, and crawls into bed.

A year to prepare, and it comes down to last-minute servicing the van. Preceded by scrambling to leave a note. The *note*. He pulls the bedcovers over his head.

He forgot to include the most important part of the note—*No Funeral*.

Trapped with his stale breath beneath the covers he's reminded of one of the many reasons he doesn't want a funeral—the perpetual mustiness permeating Summit Funeral Home. He doubts a molecule of fresh air has entered the mortuary since it was built a half a century ago. Lacking fresh oxygen to their brains might explain why staff so often misspelled names of the dearly departed using those flimsy individual letters slid into a black signboard wobbling on a stand that threatened to topple onto visitors entering the viewing area. Of all things, they'd spelled Irish's last name Heart. He'd personally removed the "e." He's sure if they had a funeral for him, his name would be incorrect as well. But he is grateful Leesie's full name had been spelled correctly. Leesie Anne Hart. And what about those paper-thin commemorative funeral leaflets? He hates having his picture taken so there aren't many photos to choose from. They'd have to crop him from a wedding picture, Irish's veil a shadow on his chin.

Gabe's thoughts travel from Summit Funeral Home down Main Street to Fallow Ridge Fellowship Hall. He'll be sure to add to the note *No Funeral or Memorial*. He imagines townsfolk, the same people who'd spend hard-earned money on standing sprays of flowers for the third Hart funeral in as many years, nibbling on fried chicken whispering, "So, it was *suicide?*"

He'd found mourner's idle mutterings at Irish's memorial, though well-intentioned, to be unbearable. He remembers seeking refuge in a small alcove off the main hall, where musty paperbacks lay scattered on a half-empty bookshelf beneath a sign, 'Leave a Book, Take a Book.' Still, he could hear the comments. *Irish was much too young. Would there never be a cure for cancer? What on earth will poor Gabe do without his sweet wife? And only two years after their little Leesie's tragic death.*

Even when mourners said goodbye to him, their palms hovered just above his shoulder, as though touching him might transfer his misfortunes onto them.

He remembers, too, sitting in his truck in the parking lot after everyone else had gone on their way. He couldn't muster the strength to turn the ignition key. On his lap he held a large envelope someone had handed him containing pictures of Irish that were displayed at the service. In the envelope was also the homemade CD with the music Irish had requested. How Irish had loved Bob Dylan. "Knockin' on Heaven's Door," a great choice.

If they *did* have a memorial for him, Gabe guesses he should just be grateful if they don't play polka music. But really, what does he care if a one-man-band performs and dances naked? He'll be long gone by then.

All that might be true, and he'll never know, but still, later that morning, he'll unseal the envelope and add to the note *P.S. No Funeral or Memorial*.

Gabe's right thumb and index finger force his tired and burning eyelids closed. He did much the same the morning Irish and he planned Leesie's funeral. However, that morning he was hoping to press his eyeballs clear through the back of his skull. The undertaker wouldn't stop talking.

Poor Mr. Bergen. His incessant conversation and planning wasn't his fault. The undertaker was just doing his job. His voice even cracked when he suggested to Gabe and Irish they forego a traditional gathering in the fellowship hall following the funeral, given the circumstances around their daughter's death. And would they agree just the immediate family for the little girl's brief graveside service?

Gabe had barely managed a nod in reply when Irish asked, "Could Miss Louisa Fern play a song from *The Wizard of Oz*?"

"Why, yes, of course. 'Somewhere Over the Rainbow,'" Mr. Bergen said. "Wonderful choice …"

"No. No, not that song." Irish interrupted. "'Follow the Yellow Brick Road.' That was Leesie's 'favorite' favorite song." Every day that summer Leesie had sung the tune while skipping from one steppingstone to the next like the utility garage was Emerald City and Destiny at her heels was Toto.

Piney Valley folks cherished Miss Louisa Fern and her musical accompaniment. The retired librarian and church organist had also been Leesie's Sunday school teacher and would babysit when Irish's family wasn't available. Her arthritic fingers no longer permitted her to play the funeral home's small organ, but he can only imagine how emotionally difficult it had been for her to play Leesie's favorite song.

Yes, imagine is the best he can do when it comes to Miss Louisa Fern or most anything pertaining to his nine-year-old daughter's funeral other than that he entered the parlor and more than a hundred people turned their heads in unison toward him, pity written on every face, and over their heads the bouquets of multicolored flowers were arranged clear to the ceiling, and the blooms' sweet, pungent fragrance overwhelmed him, and the sea of grievers parted to reveal Leesie's small white casket draped with tiny yellow rose buds, and he turned on his heel and ran to the men's room to vomit.

A wave of nausea hits Gabe from reliving the moment. He repositions the heavy cover from over his head to just under his chin. He welcomes the chill of the room on his cheeks.

The tired furnace in the basement, two floors below, had run out of fuel oil a couple days ago, so Gabe switched if off. He'd seen no need getting the tank filled until there were new owners. But now with his cheeks feeling increasingly cold, he's having second thoughts. Winters were getting progressively warmer, but Piney Valley could have an unexpected cold snap. They'd had an early frost this fall, and if the house didn't sell right away, say by mid-December, without heat, the water pipes could freeze and burst. One more chore to add to his list of things to do today–turn off the main water valve before he locks the kitchen door one final time.

One final time. No, he isn't afraid to die. He should have been buried six feet under *last* October. He would have been, too, if not for his promise. "Gabe," Irish had requested more times than he could count those final few months of her life, "just promise."

Gabe touches his stubbled cheek where a year ago he'd felt his wife's dying breath.

A thousand times over the last year he's relived that final moment. Half the time he's convinced himself Irish died an instant before he made the promise she'd been waiting—dying—to hear. In that scenario, she died not knowing he'd given his word. Other times, he's equally convinced he whispered his promise and *then* he felt the fleeting puff of warmth from her lips touch his cheek, as though she'd let go because he'd finally made his promise.

Three-hundred and sixty-five days later, he's never established the true sequence of events, and he never will.

But what does it matter, really, if it ever did? The day—*the* day—has arrived to make good on his promise to Irish. By five o'clock that afternoon, October 1, 2013, he will have kept his promise; he'll have gone to that godforsaken prison and faced the son-of-a-bitch who killed their little Leesie. No longer will he have to feel any sense of obligation to Irish or live one more unbearable day without his wife and daughter.

He'll finally be able to keep the promise he made only to himself during those distressing moments he held Irish's lifeless body, a promise she knew nothing about.

A familiar twinge in his lower spine signals sharp pain will soon follow. Gabe adjusts his hips but remains flat on his back.

"Gabe, honey." The words are nearer and softer than the cotton pillowcase cradling his head. "Roll onto your side."

## TWO

### GABE – The Big Dipper

"Irish?" For the first time in a year, her name escapes his lips in the bed they once shared.

"Irish?" He lays motionless beneath the covers, the only sounds being the pounding of his heart in his chest and Destiny's snoring in the hall where he's camped in front of Leesie's closed bedroom door.

That *was* Irish, right? That was *her* voice? Well, yes, of course, he argues with himself, he knows she's dead. So, hearing her voice is basically impossible, right? And if it's not, then he should be frightened, shouldn't he? He doesn't know, maybe, but if he's honest, he's actually feeling a sense of peace he hasn't felt, well, since he can remember.

Gabe lifts his head slightly off the pillow in case that position better enables him to catch the sound of her voice again. Silence. Then, like he's raising an antenna for better reception, he props himself fully on his elbows. "Irish, are you here?"

Balanced precariously on his elbows, straining to hear anything other than Destiny's snorts, a cold wave of panic washes over Gabe. Not fear, panic. He falls back onto the mattress. So, is that it? Just that once? Is he *again* never to hear Irish's voice ever again? He never asked for or expected to hear from her after she passed, but now that he has …

But then again, he needs to entertain the possibility he fabricated the whole thing.

His mind races like a sports car chasing an elusive checkered flag. Did he or did he not hear Irish's voice?

Her voice. So concerned about hearing her voice a second time, he's only now considering the words he heard.

The words … the words … what were the *words* he heard—or imagined? How can he not remember? Is he totally losing his mind?

His breathing grows rapid and shallow. Maybe he doesn't want to recall them. But why? he chides himself. *Think*, man. And then he remembers. "Gabe, honey, roll onto your side."

Only one person knew those words and would have spoken them—Irish. Those six words were her nightly verbal nudge to help him avoid spasms when he laid too long on his back.

Gabe sits up slowly and hugs his thighs to his chest. "Irish, I know it was you."

But with those words he suddenly feels like that lonely little kid in foster care, who would sit in bed at night hugging his knees, rocking back and forth, believing his dead mother had spoken to him.

Adult Gabe is also remembering just what a ridiculous notion *that* had been. Imagining his dead mother visited him, like an angel or a ghost, turned out to be nothing more than childhood make-believe and wishful thinking. He'd eventually outgrown the fantasy, though it did seem that once he stopped imagining his dead mother's voice, nights were spent overhearing actual adults' heated arguments from the other side of a bedroom door.

"I don't care if it's two in the morning!" one horrible man had yelled. "Get his pimple face the hell outta here!" Gabe's bedroom door had flown open and crashed against the wall. He leapt from bed into a softball-sized fist square in his gut. "Think before you leap, stupid asshole." The horrible man with putrid alcohol breath was going nose to nose with Gabe when the foster mother threw young Gabe a regretful glance as she lifted the horrible man's arm around her neck and cozied up to him, luring him out of the bedroom with a promise she'd make it worth his while. Gabe pulled on his jeans and shirt over his pjs, grabbed his black garbage bag of belongings, and ran.

Gabe's instinct to run sometimes served him well as a teen, other times not so much. And like it or not, right now he's tempted to get dressed and run. But where on earth would he go? And besides, he has promises to keep today.

He sees daylight begin to filter through the shade covering the east-facing window. He looks for The Big Dipper—the name Irish gave the ladle-like pattern of pinholes in the window shade. His back grows as straight as one of the four posters surrounding him when he notices miniscule particles of dust dancing on the beams of light streaming through the shade's pinholes. The movement of the particles reminds him of Irish. She always appeared to move effortlessly as though it was all gravity could do to keep her on the ground.

Gabe's eyes follow the shafts of daylight penetrating deeper into the room where he sees every drawer of the walnut dresser is open with his underwear and socks spilling out. The maple rocker in the corner is jammed against the faded flower-papered wall. Against the adjacent wall the paint-chipped vanity is strewn with his jeans. On the vanity mirror, a rumpled, red flannel shirt hangs by a cuff like it grabbed the nearest thing midflight. Scattered on the nightstand are decayed sunflowers.

Every item in the room—every piece of furniture and clothing — exactly where he left it the night before. *There's your proof, Gabe.* Proof Irish did *not* visit or speak to him. If she had, the Queen of Clean, even in death, could never have resisted tidying up, or, at the very least, clearing the shriveled sunflower petals off the nightstand.

Gabe's legs collapse onto the mattress like glacier ice calving into a frozen sea. For the past year, he's left everything in the room a wreck on the ghost of a chance Irish might visit. Because then if she did, he'd know because she'd have to straighten the chair, remove his shirt from the dresser mirror, and toss the sunflowers. He *knew* it was a ridiculous notion because, well, ghosts don't exist. But he always justified his actions by thinking he had nothing to lose.

So that's that. Irish didn't visit, and he didn't hear her voice. Plain and simple.

He guesses subconsciously he just *wanted* to hear her say one more time during his lifetime, "Gabe, honey, roll onto your side." But the reality is, Irish didn't speak to him any more than his dead mother had when he was a little boy, regardless of how much he'd wanted her to.

Chronic insomnia can play tricks on a person, Gabe rationalizes. Makes people see and hear things. All true, but dust particles do contain a fair amount of dead human skin, so he can *almost* justify the idea of Irish dancing about in their bedroom. But if it was Destiny's snorts he'd heard instead of Irish, he doesn't have a clue what that's all about.

What he does know is he'd give anything for Irish to snuggle up to him and remind him to roll onto his side. Anything. Gabe stares at Irish's side of the bed and rests his hand there, where it remains long after the cover no longer feels cold.

# THREE

## GABE – Splash and Dash

Gabe, aware he's lying on the mattress flat on his back again, wonders if he's trying to tempt Irish to pay a visit. Honestly, at this point, he has no earthly idea.

Hoping for distraction, Gabe studies a large cobweb dangling between two blades of the ceiling fan. Okay, point taken that he must have *cobwebs* in his head to confuse particles of dust for the ghost of Irish or thinking Destiny's snoring was Irish speaking.

He has to admit confusion and wishful thinking have become all too frequent lately. Just last week, he saw Irish's favorite dark chocolate displayed on the counter at Sulley's and bought three bars to surprise her. And a couple days ago, he drove past Leesie's school at recess half-expecting to see her in a swing on the playground.

Gabe's taken aback when a brown spider rappels from the cobweb. Well, look at that. He assumed the web was abandoned scatter. Clearly he was wrong because there's one busy spider hard at work, suspended at the end of a newly spun thread and spinning another.

Blast Irish and her "signs." Instead of a distraction, the cobweb and its unexpected inhabitant have Gabe questioning his conclusion about Irish's visit. He'd made an inaccurate first assumption about the cobweb's relevance and who's to say he isn't doing the same with Irish?

But hasn't he settled all that already? No second guessing. Irish did not appear. Remember, he tells himself, dead or alive, Irish would never tolerate the bedroom in its current state of mess. Never. And has he totally forgotten he has never believed—not really—in angels or ghosts? That in and of itself, should stamp the case closed.

But Gabe continues spying on the spider, finding it simply fascinating how it goes about its business spinning threads and leaping with abandon into the unknown. Suddenly, the spider retreats to the middle of the web where Gabe knows it will wait to feel the threads vibrate when prey helplessly fall victim.

Gabe logically understands the spider's natural instinct to be patient and use its sense of feeling to survive, but integrating it into his life is totally foreign to Gabe. He has little patience to wait for much of anything and is definitely no good at feelings.

Gabe thinks for a moment and then corrects himself that he's no good at feelings. Over the last year he's known all day long how it feels to be alone. And just this morning, less than an hour ago, for the first time in a year, he hadn't felt alone.

Gabe's temples throb. He wills his eyelids closed. Feelings are the last thing he wants to think about. Feelings are supposed to be Irish's department.

◉ ◉ ◉

She flicked on the bedside light, pushed her pillow against the headboard, and leaned back. "Sorry, I know it's two in the morning, but I can't shake a feeling, Gabe."

Still half asleep, he rolled over and kissed her shoulder. Her skin felt cool to his lips; she'd been up for a while. Even through his sleepy haze, he saw how intently Irish's big blue eyes were focused on the footboard. And she was chewing her thumbnail.

She said she couldn't explain what was worrying her, but she knew it wasn't because she doubted her husband's ability to fly a hot air balloon. So, she questioned if maybe Leesie was too young to be a passenger or if maybe NOAA had issued a weather alert.

Gabe grabbed his cellphone from his nightstand and showed Irish there were no warnings on either of the weather apps. And Leesie, he reminded her, was in third grade, plenty old enough for her first hot air balloon ride and more mature than many adults he'd flown. Besides, he reminded Irish, Tom, their balloon crew chief for years, was like an uncle to Leesie. And Jon had crewed a gazillion times and was Leesie's godfather, for heaven's sakes, so he'd throw himself in front of a bus for her if he had to. It would be a great flight. He promised.

Leesie climbed into the balloon basket at 6:30 a.m. that September morning. Gabe opened the propane valve for a long burn, and a blast of orange flame shot above their heads into the seven-story envelope. Leesie's eyes grew wide, and she giggled she was riding in the belly of a dragon. She blew kisses from the tips of her fuzzy pink gloves to Irish who was dancing in yellow Muck boots on the dewy grass. As the balloon ascended, Gabe smiled when his young daughter observed how it felt more like the earth was falling away from them than like they were being lifted. As they floated upward and then leveled off westward, she waved to a doe and fawn that leapt through a field speckled with wanna-be jack-o-lanterns and marveled how she could so clearly hear a dog's bark so far off in the distance.

Irish rode shotgun in the chase van with Tom at the wheel and Jon in the backseat. Gabe knew Irish would be relieved surface winds were so calm there couldn't have been the slightest flicker of a lit match. Still, Gabe radioed Tom more than usual reporting fuel and altimeter readings. He was hoping to put Irish's mind at ease as she'd be hanging on every word.

At five hundred feet, Lessie rested her chin on her arms crisscrossed on the basket's brown leather trim. Her eyes scanned the rolling countryside, the way a person does when they aren't really looking at anything in particular. The tilt of her head and a slight wrinkle between her eyebrows had him imagining, as he still did, what his little girl would look like all grown up.

"Hey, spunky-doodle, having fun?"

"Oh, Daddy!" She straightened until the back of her head rested against the front of his fleece vest. "We're flying like a bird! Or an angel! I thought it would feel like standing on Fallow Ridge. You know, on that big rock? But we're standing on air! Well, sort of." She shuffled around in the limited space until she could look up into his face. "Daddy, is it hard to fly?"

Gabe rambled on about the science of flight—weight, lift, thrust, and drag. He talked about how he always loved aviation and that a DC3 was his favorite plane because it's the best built aircraft ever. He went on to share that while taking lessons to become an amateur fixed-wing pilot, he'd crewed for a buddy at the world's largest hot air balloon fest, out in Albuquerque, New Mexico—did she know where New Mexico was? Yes, of course, she did—anyway, he crewed with a team handling a gigantic balloon, and huge colorful parrot, and fell flat in love with ballooning. Did she know Mommy and Daddy saved up for two years to buy their balloon? And Mommy came up with the "Top O' the Morning" shamrock on the side?

He honestly meant to answer Leesie's question, but got off on one of his tangents and never did, not really.

Still Leesie spun around 180 degrees and spread her arms to a cloudless sky. "Daddy, when I grow up, I'm going to fly, too!"

"Well, that's about the best news I've heard all day."

"Mommy tried to hide it." Leesie pulled on several strands of her long blonde curls. "She was worried about me flying this morning. She just didn't want me to know. But if we're careful, and we do our very best, everything turns out okay!"

"Leesie, how did you get to be so smart?" He kissed the top of her stocking cap. "Hey, wait till you see *this*."

Echo Pond, known for its beaver colonies, was in view. Gabe acknowledged Irish's words of caution, but conditions were ideal for a splash and dash. As they neared the pond where several felled trees littered the bank, he pointed out a large beaver lodge thick with layers of mud and sticks to Leesie. One of the furry rodents whapped its huge tail on the surface of the water and scurried to safety. Leesie called out, "We're not really a dragon! Please don't be afraid!"

Gabe pulled the red vent line to release heat from the envelope, and in less than a minute they had descended until the bottom of the basket skimmed along the top of the water.

"Splash and dash!" Gabe shouted over the roar of another prolonged burn. "You don't have to remember all this now, sweetheart. But it takes 45 seconds for a balloon to react to the heat from a burn." Closing the valve, he continued in a normal voice. "Now we have enough lift to clear that tree line."

They rose quietly above the water, and Leesie glanced from the ripples now far beneath them to the autumn-colored wooded area they were approaching. "Daddy, I want to fly—"

"Oh, sweetheart, just a sec. You'll learn this, too." The underside of the basket grazed the treetops of the wooded area. "Feel how you can use tree branches to slow down the balloon? That's so we can land over there, in that big field. Oh, look, there's the chase van. And Mommy running to greet us."

Gabe prepared for touchdown as the basket glided across the trees and approached the abandoned field that he and Tom had previously identified as a good landing site. No high-tension wires as far as the eye could see. And no low-profile electric—Gabe saw the oxidized lines hidden in the large stand of trees in the southwest corner of the field at the exact moment Tom, out of breath from running, radioed the news.

He and Tom concurred landing was committed at that point and the electric lines would not be an issue, positioned far enough down the field to safely land and maneuver the balloon. Tom reported winds were not predicted to pick up for at least another hour. Should be a smooth landing, still Tom and Jon—and Irish—were ready and anxious to catch the basket.

Just as a precaution, Gabe instructed Leesie to sit on the basket floor in the corner and hug her knees. Knowing Irish would have said something to make everything appear normal—which it was, he added that passengers sometimes sit during landing to give the pilot more room to move around.

Pulling the red vent line for initial descent, Gabe measured by seconds the amount of air released from the balloon. The vent line still in one hand, where it would remain the duration of the flight, he leaned over the edge of the basket to read the tree branches beneath them. The only leaves rustling where those the basket strategically swept across.

Gabe hit the burner with small bursts of heat as the inverted teardrop-shaped balloon gracefully cleared the tree line and the ground crew eagerly moved into position to catch the basket.

The wind shear came out of nowhere. The massive balloon, filled with 77,000 cubic feet of hot air, wobbled and dipped like a party balloon. The crew of three watched from the field in disbelief as the seventy-foot-tall inflatable rolled forty-five degrees.

Inside the basket, Gabe pulled the vent line to release additional air from the balloon to speed descent and slow momentum.

The sudden burst of wind had shifted their flight trajectory; they were heading toward the southwest corner of the field. He had to set the balloon down, now.

Tom, Jon, and Irish were approaching the basket when another burst, an updraft, threatened to relaunch the balloon.

With a round turn and double-half hitch, Gabe secured his end of the drop line to the stainless-steel frame of the basket and dropped the other end of the line over the edge to Tom. The line swung just out of Tom's reach, so he leapt and grabbed it with leather-gloved hands while Gabe pulled with his full weight on the red line to fully deploy the parachute vent. Seconds felt like hours.

The balloon descended, finally. The forward motion caused the wicker basket to hit the ground with a thud and skid. To further slow the balloon, the crew of three jumped on the downwind side of the basket, their arms draped over the leather trim. All three knew, however, the basket wasn't yet on the ground for good. The balloon's momentum at touchdown caused it to rise again, lifting the basket three feet off the ground.

Irish lost her grip and fell onto the field. But she jumped up, and without brushing herself off ran alongside the basket, her blue eyes intent on it with the fierce resolve of a mother ready to snatch her child from what Leesie had affectionately described as a dragon. At the first opportunity, Irish squeezed in between Tom and Jon and grabbed hold of the edge of the basket and seemed to with every ounce of her being command the fiery beast to stop, and it did.

Irish, Tom, and Jon looked wide-eyed at each other and then at Gabe before cheering for the little girl huddled in the corner of the basket. "We have touchdown! Happy first flight, Leesie!"

Leesie jumped up from the basket floor, beaming from ear to ear, and wrapped her arms around Gabe. "Thank you, Daddy! You're the best balloon pilot *ever!*"

"Hey, yeah ... " What else could he say with pieces of his heart stuck in his throat.

Still shaken, Gabe managed to lift his daughter to sit on the edge of the basket while Tom and Jon collapsed the balloon envelope. Irish caressed Leesie's cheeks and kissed them both.

"Mommy! Mommy!" Leesie's eyes were even bigger and bluer than her mother's. "Remember you said girls can be astronauts? Daddy and I talked a lot about it when we were flying. And, when I get big, I'm going to be an *astronaut!*"

An astronaut? Gabe, still trying to catch his breath, was puzzled. Leesie said she wanted to be a hot air balloon pilot! Where in the world did *astronaut* come from? Being an astronaut was never even mentioned.

But, Gabe realized, Leesie hadn't mentioned becoming a hot air balloon pilot either.

Irish explained to Gabe later that day the whole astronaut conversation. A few nights before, Leesie had spotted her first satellite. Leesie followed the satellite's track with her finger and asked nonstop questions about missiles and rockets and outer space. Irish had done the best she could to explain a subject she knew little about, other than the moon landing in '69 and space stations somewhere—she waved—out there.

◉ ◉ ◉

Gabe opens his eyes and checks on the crafty spider above him. That spider has to stay two steps ahead of its prey. And he's not saying Irish was a spider, for God's sakes, but how, Gabe wonders, did she always seem to be two steps ahead of life? Was it because she felt her way through her existence? She'd had a feeling about Leesie's first balloon ride, though she couldn't articulate it. Still, she was right to be anxious, and to share her concerns with him. And he did listen, even though he thought she was worrying needlessly.

Out of the blue, watching the spider, Gabe is reminded just how much he loved Spider Man as a kid—the superhero was an orphan, just like him, but had superpowers to clean up crime and avenge his uncle's murder.

Gabe wishes he possessed a superpower to avenge Leesie's murder.

Right. He's nowhere close to superhuman. Irish, however, well, she sort of was. Her extraordinary talent for listening to her feelings and to her heart drove him crazy at times, but she clearly had a gift.

Yet as gifted as Irish was at acknowledging her feelings, Gabe's childhood had been difficult, causing him to navigate life and emotions differently. In a way, he'd had to summon special powers *not* to succumb to his feelings. When he was really young in foster care, he'd allowed his emotions to surface. But more times than not, his feelings were torpedoed like a submarine and sunk to the bottom of his heart.

Like that crazy lop-eared mutt chained to a doghouse in a mud hole of a backyard belonging to a family he stayed with when he was eight years old. Gabe would sneak out after dark to feed it scraps when the family forgot to take it food or punished it for barking. He never saw the family play with the dog or call him by a name, so Gabe named him Snoopy. The pup would jump with joy, and his tail would wag like crazy when he'd see Gabe steal into the yard to be with him. They were both abandoned, but still there for each other. Gabe laid in bed some nights with one hand on his bag of clothes, plotting how he and Snoopy would run away.

At sunrise one morning a social worker came into Gabe's room and had him get dressed, then ushered him out the front door of the house and into a white van. Gabe opened a side van window and called, "Bye, Snoopy," then wished he hadn't. What if Snoopy barked? He might not get food that day. Gabe needn't have worried. There was no bark.

The van had begun to move down the street, and for an instant Gabe thought he saw Snoopy flying his doghouse, just like in the comics, over the dilapidated backyard fence and into a thick, white cloud. But, of course, he hadn't *really* seen the mutt flying his doghouse. That morning, riding alone in the backseat of that van, realizing he hadn't gotten to pet Snoopy goodbye, Gabe decided the whole caring thing hurt too much. His feelings stayed submerged until Irish.

She was like a deep-sea treasure hunter salvaging sunken cache, reclaiming more pieces of Gabe's heart than he ever knew he possessed.

Irish said for her it was love at first sight. For Gabe, when he spotted her in the main hall at Piney Valley High, he thought she was attractive enough with her long blonde hair and crystal blue eyes. But then she spoke to him. She asked him about an upcoming assembly in such a way that he felt of all the students in school she was asking *him* because he was the *only* one who knew the answer. And the way she tilted her head and looked up at him with those eyes, just the right amount of dreamy, he fell in love with not only her, but a little with himself.

If he could have that kind of effect on such a brilliant and beautiful girl, well, maybe he wasn't as unlovable as he always believed.

Just another example of Irish's superpower—getting him to believe in himself. Then there was the afternoon a few weeks later, before football practice, when she was waiting for him outside the boy's locker room, her books held close to her chest. Her eyes were intent on him as he walked toward her, and she was nervously biting on her thumbnail. He knew it; she wanted to break up with him. He was prepared to stuff his feelings so his heart wouldn't break in two.

Her blue eyes pierced right through him when she said, "Gabe, I have something to tell you. And I'm really not sure how to say it." The pain in his chest was unbearable. "I hope you understand and that you don't think I'm being silly. See, well, I have a funny feeling."

What kind of breakup tactic was *that*? Gabe had never seriously dated before so he had no experience getting dumped, but just break up already, he thought. Why does she have to twist the knife?

"Maybe double-check your football helmet."

"What? *What?*"

"Yes, I know. You're right. I'm just being a worrywart. But, could you humor me and just be careful during practice today?"

"You mean you're not breaking up with me?"

"Breaking up with you? Are you out of your mind? I'm in *love* with you!"

"You're … *what?*" Gabe hugged her, told her he loved her, too, and floated out onto the football field.

Not 30 minutes later, under a perfectly clear sky, a rogue bolt of lightning struck the center of the team huddle. Two players were knocked back several feet, and Gabe sustained minor burns to the bottoms of his feet.

Irish never said I told you so. That wasn't a thing with Irish. It was just when she had a strong feeling, she was lousy at hiding it.

She'd been so right about the balloon ride—to trust her feelings. If there'd been another windshear or if Irish had not been able to grab the basket a second time or if Leesie had panicked, well, he didn't need to think about that right now.

Gabe's gut aches. He needs to focus on the spider. He knows when he gets in this kind of mental loop, he has to let it go. But this morning has been too much. He can't let go—where the hell were Irish's *feelings* the morning Leesie was killed? How could she not have *some* inkling a drunk driver would mow down their daughter right in front of their house?

Gabe hates himself when his thoughts go to that place of blaming Irish for what happened to their daughter. But he's just too exhausted to fight it right now. If there is a plus side to being upset about Irish's lack of *feelings* the morning Leesie died, right now he less wants to hear from or see his late wife.

# FOUR

## IRISH – Earth Bound

Grandmother Lord cautioned, her clear blue eyes behind her wire-rimmed glasses looking beyond me and into my maiden voyage back to Earth, "Old habits die hard, Irish."

"I promise, Grandmother," I teased her, "I won't do anything to make you roll over in your grave."

"Irish," she scolded, lovingly, like she'd done a million times when I was a little and acting silly, the *ish* of my name pronounced more like shush. "Sometimes," Grandmother added, "sometimes old habits, they don't die at all."

◉ ◉ ◉

So consumed with imagining myself back on Earth, in whatever form that might be, I never considered *how* I might get there. Yes, it was a crazy ride, and though it appeared to Gabe as a meteor traveling hundreds of miles overhead at thousands of miles per hour, the experience for me was like a blink of an eye.

In a blink of an eye, I was standing in our bedroom, waiting for Gabe to come into the house from the utility garage. In another blink of an eye, Gabe was lying in bed flat on his back. Another blink, I was close enough to him to whisper, "Gabe, honey, roll onto your side."

◉ ◉ ◉

Yes, Grandmother's words about old habits had echoed in my head. As did Charles and Mary Esther's thoughts about Gabriel as a little boy, how he seemed to ache to accept whispers from the beyond, but resisted truly believing his dead mother, or father, could speak to him.

Their son had only been a toddler when they'd died, far too young for them to have shared with him he'd been named after the archangel Gabriel. (I'd always wondered!) Still, they'd hoped because of the origin of his name he'd instinctively accept the appearance of angels.

But as Gabriel grew into his teens, he resisted even more his parents' attempts to reach out to him. So instead, they'd wait at the street curb until their son was safely inside a new foster home or watch to see if in the cafeteria line at school he took an extra helping of his favorite meal. "Meatballs and spaghetti with garlic bread!" the three of us smiled and chimed in unison.

"Gabriel is still too thin," his mother had added, "just like when he was young."

The last person to school me this morning about my visit had been Uncle Grover. Chin tilted upward and thumbs hooked into the front pockets of his serge wool vest, he said, in the most pathetic imitation of an Irish brogue ever, "Irish Eyes, your job this day is to be the thread that weaves the tapestry of all that transpires." Maybe I inherited my love of foolishness from him because he's the silliest man you'd ever hope to meet, and his wink confirmed he was looking for my laugh. I didn't disappoint. But I also knew he'd been serious with his words.

Thing is, I don't know how to be a "thread" or encourage Gabe to eat without speaking to him or doing *something*.

◉ ◉ ◉

*It was one year to the day after she died. I was alone, no umbrella, my tears mixing with a fine mist, falling to my knees on the damp earth that would forever separate me from my daughter. I sensed a presence and turned, assuming Gabe had followed me to the cemetery. The only person about was a caretaker in the distance, on a knoll, dressed in a gray rain slicker, laboring to push a wheelbarrow.*

*At first, I thought I was possibly having a stroke. I couldn't feel the cold or drizzle on the right side of my face. My mouth went bone dry, and her name barely passed my lips before everything went black. Leesie's glove against my cheek felt as soft and fuzzy as I'd remembered. And hearing "Mommy" filled me with joy that even surpassed the time her chubby hand wrapped around my finger and two short nonsensical babbles first formed the word "mama."*

*I was awakened by a nudge on my shoulder; the caretaker said he saw me go down. I learned his name was William, and after that day, he took it upon himself to look out for me whenever I visited Leesie's grave alone.*

*At the time, I didn't share with anyone, not even Gabe, what transpired that day. I suppose because I didn't want to appear hysterical, but more so because for some reason, I needed to feel a connection with my daughter no one else ever could, like the bond we had when I alone carried her in my womb, feeding her and tolerating her thrashing about and causing me heartburn. For a moment, it had again been just Leesie and me.*

◉ ◉ ◉

So, yes, I know how frightening and confusing it can be to hear from the other side. That reason, and only that reason is why I should remain silent. Staying silent has never been my strong suit—anyone who knows me can attest. Like Grandmother cautioned, "Old habits die hard," but from time to time I've held my tongue.

◉ ◉ ◉

*"Well, sweetie, some people call them that, but they aren't really 'shooting stars,'" Gabe corrected Leesie where they sat together on the back porch steps watching a meteor shower, their heads titled identically. I watched the two of them from just inside the kitchen door as Gabe further explained. "You see, stars are made of gas, and these streaks of light are from meteors—think of space rocks—falling to Earth."*

*"Cool!" Leesie cheered. "Space rocks!" Then she cocked her head and asked, "But they can sometimes be angels, right? Grandma says sometimes they can be angels."*

*"Oh, spunky doodle." Gabe wrapped his arm around Leesie's shoulder and lightly kissed the top of her head. "No, honey. Meteors can't be angels."*

*Leesie studied Gabe's face like she might ask another question, but then snuggled into her daddy's hug.*

◉ ◉ ◉

None of us knew, or were supposed to know, the foreshadowing of Leesie's question about meteors and angels. I'd had my opinion that evening (I believed it very possible), but said nothing, and honestly was surprised that I didn't say something. Even when Gabe looked over his shoulder at me and motioned for me to join them, I waved and returned to the dishes.

I've thought about that moment as many times as Gabe has relived making his promise to me.

And, yes, Gabe saw an angel tonight—not a *meteor*, as he believed, but no words or actions will ever convince him of that. And yet he is right, a meteor can't be an angel, but an Earth-bound angel often looks like a meteor to a mortal stargazer.

Like Uncle Grover advised, my job is not to alter or even influence Gabe's reactions or decisions. (Otherwise, he would *not* still be on his back!) My husband has free will.

What I *can* do, if the most important man in my once real life and now afterlife will allow me, is to ease his sense of hopelessness as he navigates the day's memories, struggles, and frustrations. How do I do that? I guess just being present with the knowledge that Gabe will forever try to find the logic in everything. "Old habits die hard … and sometimes, they don't die at all."

Speaking of old habits, as I look around this mess of a bedroom, who's going to help *me*? I knew the room would be a wreck, but given my heavenly attributes, I thought I'd simply shrug off the fact that dirty clothes are *not* in the laundry basket and year-old sunflower remnants are *still* on the nightstand.

I've been in such a remarkable place this last year. Not a tiptoe-through-the-clouds kind of place. Not an I've-got-it-all-figured-out kind of place. It's a *kind* kind of place. A place not made of perfection, but goodwill, where you would naturally expect to find people like Mother Teresa, Anne Frank, and Martin Luther King Jr, but there are also folks with the hearts of volunteer crossing guards, whistling grocery clerks, nurses, first responders, and everyone's pets.

The kindness I experience where I now reside is not dissimilar from that on Earth. The difference is that on Earth, kindness is not always seen as a constant. Too often people on Earth react to a situation like convicts escaping down a laundry shoot, with no thought of consequences.

I've been in that unworldly, dare I say heavenly place for a year, so to now have mortal struggles and emotions, like desires of the flesh, tug at me is unexpected and unsettling. Gabe's aliveness washes over me. His scent fills the room in the bed we shared, made love in, snuggled in as a family on lazy Saturday mornings, the bed where I died one year ago this morning. Who knew angels could ache in the most unexpected places?

I don't dare touch him, not even one strand of his hair, which of course is in crazy need of a cut. His hair's been a shaggy mess for 36 years or at least since we met in high school. But that's part of what makes him so incredibly irresistible to me.

And that jawline, a chin so near perfection, it's worthy of Michelangelo's chisel, though Gabe would challenge the master that he didn't have the perspective quite right or the subject posed so the light hits at the right angle.

Headstrong? Opinionated? You *think?* He debated everything from a simple haircut to what today should mean to me. And what I'd hoped it would mean to him. It was a contest right up until the end.

My last day on Earth, I awoke (regained consciousness is a better way to describe it) to Gabe towering beside the bed and Miss Jane at his side, MJ's head barely coming up to his shoulder. Gabe's face lit up, and I could tell he thought I was back for good. But it was MJ's eyes I trusted. She had nursed patients like me for three decades. As it turned out, I'd been no different than countless others—patients near death rallying one final time to utter parting words or hear a long-awaited promise.

Months before, Gabe and I had read the hospice materials. We both knew about the dying surge of energy. Gabe, however, disregarded most everything in the pamphlets. He refused to update our wills, or to buy the two cemetery plots next to Leesie's, or to discuss my memorial service with my dad. Stubborn.

And now, seeing him here flat on his back, I'm convinced his willfulness holds him in that position. He *knows* he should roll onto his side, but he won't do it. It would seem he'd rather suffer.

But, honestly, who really knows why a person reacts the way they do when they're grieving? God knows my judgment was clouded beyond belief after we lost Leesie. It's hard to believe now that I entered her classroom unannounced the Monday morning after she died and sat in her chair, running my fingers over names carved into the wooden desktop looking for my daughter's, and removed her books and #2 pencil while Ms. Grant diverted the children to the cafeteria, and the principal sat in a pupil's desk close by and consoled me before escorting me to my car. My actions were inexcusable. Each child, I'm sure, was already traumatized by learning from their parents over the weekend that their classmate would not be returning to school Monday morning or ever.

By comparison, what Gabe did in those last moments before I died was such a small thing, but I'm reminded of it now looking at our bedroom window. I'd been in a coma in a dark room for days, and moments after I'd finally opened my eyes, Gabe raised the window shade.

"I know how much you love the autumn colors and light," he announced.

I managed a hint of a smile. It wasn't worth the effort, nor did I have the strength to tell him how insensitive he was being, that the daylight was more than I could tolerate.

I didn't stay with that thought long because it was then I noticed MJ remove her sterile gloves. The perfunctory act, stretching and folding each elastic glove into itself set me into a panic. The removing of her gloves represented to me that everything and anything she could do had been done. My fate was no longer in the hands of medicine.

Her medical skills surpassed only by her compassion, MJ tenderly rested her hand on my arm. I was so grateful for that warm human touch of a knowing hand. I understood then that's why she'd removed the gloves. That simple act of kindness helped me realize that everything—whatever everything might be—would be all right.

MJ's eyes softened, seeing me at ease again, and with a gentle squeeze on my arm, she turned to Gabe and excused herself so we could be alone.

Gabe eased himself onto the edge of the bed and whispered, "Until you woke up, I thought you'd … I thought I'd lost you … too." The corners of his mouth raised ever so slightly as someone does when they're hoping beyond all hope.

His gaze moved from me to the east window and extended far past Fallow Ridge, as though into our future together. The silver at his temples, I remember thinking, had not been there two years before, nor had the slump of his shoulders or furrows fixed across his brow like rows of headstones lined in a cemetery.

"Gabe," I whispered, "just promise, just promise me."

An act of distraction rather than care, Gabe tucked the blanket around my shoulders.

"You have to promise." I looked into the coffee-brown eyes I'd fallen in love with the first time they'd glanced my way. "If you don't promise and keep it, I know you'll … I worry that you'll …"

Gabe's body straightened, his arms across his chest so I tried another approach. "You're … too … too young … to give up. To not even try."

"Oh, but it's okay for *you*," he snapped.

"Accepting," I whispered, "is not giving up."

Gabe's broad shoulders caved. He buried his face in my pillow, his hair—unwashed and musky—brushed my cheek. I tried to will my hand to comfort him like MJ's touch had me, but not one finger would so much as twitch. I prayed for the right words. "Leesie spoke to me."

Gabe shot upright. "What? Irish, what are you talking about?"

"I heard her voice, Gabe. Briefly. But if I lived to be 200, the sound would be with me."

"You're talking crazy." He looked away with a wave of his hand. "It's all that medicine they have you on."

"No. No. It was not long after we lost her. Gabe, it was Leesie. It was our little Leesie."

Gabe leapt to his feet and scanned the room like a madman. Finally, he seized the glass vase filled with sunflowers off the nightstand, water splashing out and onto the hardwood floor. The way he aimed the vase at the wall, I expected to hear a shattering of glass at any moment. But Gabe took pause like a baseball pitcher mid-throw, second-guessing the catcher's signal. His arm shook. His whole torso shuddered. Finally, his bristly chin dipped, his arm dropped, and, using both hands to steady, he slid the vase back onto the table.

He grabbed a flannel shirt off the footboard and dabbed at the water on the floor. After he threw the shirt in the direction of the vanity table, he lifted himself onto the bed next to me. I felt his breath, his tears.

"Oh, Irish, I'm sorry, I'm sorry, Irish, I .. I just … "

I wished then the life in his body could feed mine and the peace in my heart could ease his.

Had it been in my power, I'd have stayed as long as it took. But I couldn't. I couldn't wait—with or without Gabe's promise.

When I finally let go, I found myself grateful to sink into contentedness as I felt myself rise. I remember smiling, knowing the last word I spoke aloud to my husband was our precious daughter's name.

And then, there it was in the stillness beyond silence. Not a moment too soon, Gabe's whisper. "I promise."

# FIVE

## COODER – A Falling Star

Cooder Ward lay on the narrow mattress, one elbow against the cold concrete wall, wishing that instead of a dark cracked ceiling he was staring up at a starlit sky. There was a time, when the prison doctors said he'd be blind within two years, that he doubted he'd ever again see the Big Dipper or the Milky Way. Yep, he reckons he'd have missed seeing the stars about more than anything. Well, not more than Charlene. Or Irish. Or, of course, Momma.

◉ ◉ ◉

*Her toes pulled at tall blades of crabgrass as they rocked in the metal glider. He'd turned six that summer but Momma still carried him outdoors from his bed saying it was just too darn hot to sleep. Rubbing his eyes, he was afraid it meant it was too hot for him to snuggle up to her, but she didn't seem to mind. He about fell asleep again, there next to her, when Momma stopped the glider and* said, "Look! It's a falling star!" She held his head and aimed his nose at more specks of light than his summer batch of freckles. "Quick, Cooder, make a wish!"

He didn't look quick enough or at the right place because he didn't see the star. He wasn't about to tell Momma though. She was so excited, he knew she wanted him to be happy, too. So, he squeezed his eyes closed and suspended his legs out in front of him. His wish: Please make me tall enough so's I can push Momma in the glider.

He kept his eyes closed and, not knowing how long it might take for his skin and bones to grow, silently counted to 20. He was relieved there wasn't any pain or pulling and tugging at his legs. Finally, he reached that magical number, bent his knees and slowly lowered his feet toward the ground.

◉ ◉ ◉

"Cooder. Hey, Coo! Know you're 'wake. Need a smoke."

◉ ◉ ◉

Even with his big toes stretched down as far as they'd go, he still couldn't reach the tallest blade of grass. In fact, he wasn't sure but what his legs hadn't shrunk a little.

He was sadder than a dog short-chained to an outhouse. He sat there, his legs still, hoping Momma wouldn't notice.

◉ ◉ ◉

"Hey, man, I asked you a question! I need a smoke. Coo!"

Cooder ignores the so-called question and Bo's bare foot patting on the floor of the adjacent cell and his fingers tapping against the iron bars.

◉ ◉ ◉

*Before too long Momma started stroking his summer-cropped hair. Her touch and the smell of her cherry-scented hand lotion made him feel better right away. Momma always had a way of making everything okay.*

*He looked up at her face. She was still staring at the sky, but a tiny trail of tears ran down her cheek. Even though she couldn't have known what he'd wished for, he got it in his head she was disappointed in him, being his legs hadn't grown. He made himself a promise then and there that never again would he let his momma down. Not never.*

◉ ◉ ◉

"I mean it, Coo, I can tell when you're awake."

Cooder crosses his arms under his head and continues staring at the gray concrete ceiling above him.

*"Cooder, do you know what a falling star is?" Momma's voice was soft and low. He wasn't sure how to answer her question. So far that night he hadn't done so good with falling star stuff.* "No, Momma," *he said above the sound of crickets filling the night.* "A falling star … " *she said, like a prayer, her arm moist, but feeling like velvet wrapped around his bare shoulders,* "a falling star is an angel on a mission."

◉ ◉ ◉

"Cooder Ward, I need a cigarette now, man!"

"I quit. 'member?"

"Well, crap."

Cooder hears the thump of something hitting the other side of the shared wall. Probably a shoe, Cooder thinks. Or a fist. He rolls onto his side and peers out beneath the pancake-thin pillow now covering his baldhead.

A blast of fluorescent light floods the sector followed by a deafening reveille siren, and Cooder's feet instinctively hit the cold floor.

"Coo. Sorry, just need a cig. Hey, man, anyways, good luck. You know, today."

"Yeah. I know. Thanks, Bo."

# SIX

## GABE – Angle of the Sun

Billy Wabash's truck backfires before it rattles down the long, steep driveway. Folks around Fallow Ridge, including Gabe, marvel how the retired-postman-turned-paperboy has perfected wrapping a newspaper within itself. Most days the projectile arrives before daybreak sounding like a meteorite crashing on the front porch.

This morning Gabe's slow to sort out what caused the racket. The newspaper's loud arrival awoke him from the deepest sleep he's had in three years. Rubbing his eyes, he glances at the cobweb above his head then turns his focus to the east window shade. The angle of the sun on the maple leaves canopying the front yard causes the shade's thin fabric to glow bright orange. What time is it anyway? Only one reason the paper's this late—truck trouble. Gabe regrets he'll never know if Wabash reached his goal to rack a million miles on the Ram's original diesel engine.

Gabe props himself on one elbow and reexamines the bedroom. Still a mess.

He slides one foot toward the edge of the mattress in an attempt to get up, but sleep was intoxicating. He wants more. He lowers back onto the mattress, closes his eyes, and crosses his wrists on his forehead.

There's a theory, he knows, that once a person devises a plan to end his or her life, and once the end is near, they may finally experience a sense of the serenity that eluded them until that time, despite their best efforts. The concept makes sense to him now and explains why he slept so soundly.

That, and he's covered all the bases regarding his demise. That's a relief. He'd overlooked a couple of things—writing a note and preparing the van, of all things—but he's remedied both with time to spare.

Just think. After five o'clock this afternoon, he'll no longer need to rationalize, organize, or apologize for his life. Death suddenly seems almost too simple.

But that isn't fair—death itself might be simple, but preparing for it never is. Irish wished to die in her own bed, but he'd complicated things by insisting hospice set up a hospital bed in the living room. Irish tolerated the situation for about a week, then asked to please be carried back upstairs to their bed. Two days later she'd slipped into a coma.

He'd been so angry with her for not trying harder to live. When she awoke on what would have been Leesie's birthday, he honestly thought she'd beaten the odds. But it felt like she'd only awakened to hear him make his promise.

And then what a way for him to learn Leesie had spoken to Irish from the grave. What if Irish hadn't awakened that morning, he would never have known about her moment with their deceased little girl. Oh, and she'd only shared it with him so he'd finally make her the promise.

He remembers the glass vase with the sunflowers had been heavier than he'd expected when he'd grabbed it that morning. What he'd expected to do with it then, he still has no idea. The whole ordeal with Leesie speaking to Irish had triggered a fight-or-flight response in him, a reaction he was all too familiar with during childhood, sometimes running away in the middle of the night to keep himself from striking out in anger.

That morning with Irish, he'd just not known what to do with all that rage, having spent two years hoping beyond hope to hear his daughter's voice. Which he knew was ridiculous. But, instead Leesie choose to speak to her mother. All he's ever wanted was a simple, "Hi, Daddy!" or "I miss you, Daddy!"

Every fiber of his being aches to hear his daughter's voice, especially today.

Therein lies the rub, he reminds himself, trying to shift from anger to logic. He *doesn't believe* in angels or ghosts, but he expects to hear his deceased daughter's voice? What about earlier that morning, the nonexistent whisper from Irish and deceptive dancing dust?

Thing is, when it comes to Leesie, he *wants* to believe in angels. And now this morning, thinking of Irish, even though she can still infuriate him, Gabe doubly wants to believe in angels.

But, Gabe, angels don't exist, he reminds himself again.

Like it or not, reality was Irish didn't visit him from the other side. He might have to remind himself of that until the day—the hour—he dies.

And because angels don't exist, Irish *never* actually heard Leesie. Irish simply imagined a voice, like he had this morning. In all fairness, he could understand why Irish had been so adamant that she heard their daughter's voice. He'd been pretty convinced himself this morning that he'd heard his late wife's whisper.

Funny, even if he *did* hear Leesie's voice right now, would he believe it? Given what happened this morning, maybe not, but he'd still give anything to find out. Especially today, to hear her sweet innocent voice, real or unreal, before he makes his final walk to the utility garage, locks the door, and starts the van's engine to end his miserable life ...

Tears burn his eyes. He pounds his fists on his forehead. What if Leesie discovers her daddy took his own life? How has he never *considered* that? *Leesie, oh, sweetie, please say something, anything. If you do, sweetie, I promise not to do anything. I promise. Please just say something ...*

He grabs his hair in desperation wanting to pull out every strand. A father begs his little daughter to speak to him from the other side, so he won't *kill* himself?

He was supposed to be Leesie's protector—not accuser. Now, whether he takes his life or not, he's screwed. If he chooses to live, every day he'll have to face the fact he is the kind of man who begs his daughter to save him from taking his life. *Leesie, oh, Leesie, Daddy's so sorry ...*

God, how much easier life was when he didn't question death, when he *knew* once you died, you were gone. Poof. Forever. That the living owed the dead nothing, and the dead have no obligation to the living. Angels, ghosts, whatever people might call them, are fabrications for those left behind who are too weak to let go of the past.

As a kid he'd imagined how his life could have been different if his parents had lived. Sometimes at night he'd imagined he heard them whisper to him. Every time he had, though—oh, God. He's just realizing, every time he thought he heard his parents' voices, he ended up blaming himself that he lived, and they hadn't.

Feelings of shame he hadn't experienced, or at least acknowledged, since he was a kid were now nearly taking his breath. Now, for a second time in his life, out of a family of three, he is the only one left living. *They should all be alive, not him.*

He remembers the only way he ever moved past those feelings of shame as a kid was to simply deny the existence of afterlife and angels. He cut emotional ties to his parents, as best he could, and looked to logic to guide him. He learned there is only so much pain—and shame—he can tolerate. Reasoning saved him as a young adult, but now, alone a second time, with those he loved the most gone forever, he is just too tired to rally any more logic. Well, other than the logical end to his pain which requires him to no longer exist.

Why, he wonders, had he worried that Leesie would find out her daddy took his life? Why did he think she'd ever know he'd begged her to speak to him and save him from taking his life?

The afterlife doesn't exist, he reminds himself. Nor angels. Regardless what Irish heard. Or what he thinks he heard.

◉ ◉ ◉

"Gabe, honey, roll onto your side."

"Any *special* reason you want me on my side?" It was their wedding night, and as he turned onto his side, he ran his hand over the sheet covering her body. The soft, roundedness of Irish's breasts stirred him a second time that night.

Irish rolled to face him, and beneath the covers placed the palm of her hand on his lower spine. His back muscles relaxed even more with her warm, tender touch.

"Gabe, I don't know how you could lie there on your back in pain. You groaned and twitched like you were possessed by the devil, until you rolled on your side—thanks to me. I'm no physical therapist, but maybe don't lay flat on your back if it hurts so much from that old football injury."

"Your wish is my command, Irish Hart. Wanna know my wish? That I die in your arms, lying on my side."

Her hand slipped further down his back and her silky leg rested along his thigh. Her lips were soft and moist against his ear.

"Well, let's hope that's decades and decades from now. Until then, just don't expect this reaction from me *every* night you sleep on your back."

◎ ◎ ◎

Gabe's hands fell asleep crossed on his forehead, and the prickly feeling in his fingers snaps him back to reality. He imagines wearing weighted sparring gloves as he tries to move his hands to the mattress on either side of him.

Maybe losing Irish would have been easier if she'd reacted less to his invitations after they'd lost Leesie, or he'd become unresponsive to her touch. Or if those half-dozen words, "Gabe, honey, roll onto your side," hadn't been so much a part of their bedtime ritual, much like their three-in-a-row kisses good night.

Maybe *then* he wouldn't be so hell bent on leaving this damn world. God, there he is again, blaming someone else for the decision he's made to end his life.

Truth is his decision has nothing to do with angels or afterlife. Or Leesie or Irish. He just can't live with any more pain and disappointment. He's too tired of trying to function day after day with unbearable loneliness and hopelessness. He's tired of trying to act like normal people.

Yes, he should have ended it all a year ago. But Irish wouldn't listen to logic. She had to go and donate her eyes and make him promise to visit—

His frustration grows thinking about Irish and the corneal transplant. Feeling having returned to his hands, he reaches to knock the sunflowers off the nightstand. They are gone.

# SEVEN

## COODER – Quarter-Moon Dimples

Cooder starts at the rapid-fire clank of cell doors mechanically unlocking and sliding open. He has no appetite. But if he sees Charlene today, she'll ask if he's eaten anything, so he steps from his cell into line with the other inmates on Row H. He glances over his shoulder. He guesses Bo was skipping breakfast. Cooder's relieved.

Bo is a pain-in-the-ass. But on the inside, the pain-in-the-ass regularly saves Cooder's butt. For 38 years on the outside, Cooder had felt like an outcast. Even with Charlene and Momma, he never let them know the real Cooder. Truth is, he's not sure who the real Cooder is. So, he does and says what he thinks others expected. He once worked on construction with a guy who couldn't read. Cooder caught on to him, how the guy would wait to see how others reacted to what they'd read—notices on the bulletin board, work orders, things of that nature—then he'd respond. Cooder never gave away the guy's secret and tried to help when he could, never letting on he was onto the fact his coworker couldn't read.

Cooder sort of understood how the guy felt. Cooder always pays attention, too, to see what he should do and say depending on what others did and said.

He'll never tell Charlene, but the day the judge announced Cooder's prison sentence, he half looked forward to 20 years of not having to deal much with people. He knew he'd miss Charlene more than anything, and there was a risk she'd finally give up on him, but he was just tired of trying to act like normal people.

Prison, however, is nothing like he'd imagined. Sure, you can be a loner. But you have to look around every corner. You need survival skills. Bo warned him early on that convicts are like a pack of hyenas. They smell fear and take down the weak prisoners.

Cooder almost admires how Bo seems born for prison. Not like those hyena inmates. Bo has a *good* bad reputation on Row H. He's fair as long as the other guy's fair, too. Step out of line—Cooder's seen it happen a time or two—and Bo could make a five-year prison sentence feel like life. Bo isn't mean exactly, just fearless.

It's been 36 months since Bo, who'd been assigned to intake new prisoners that day, handed Cooder his first orange jumpsuit. Cooder thought he saw the same guilt he felt looking back at him out of the eyes of the guy with the skull tattoo on his left cheek.

Since that first day, Cooder's overheard inmates comparing him and Bo, since Bo's also doing time for hit-and-run.

Bo's victim, though, had been a 70-year-old woman wheeling her six-month-old grandson in a baby buggy. They were in a crosswalk, story goes, halfway to the other side of the street in broad daylight. Bo was driving and tipping a paper bag to get that last drop and never saw them.

Witnesses said the grandmother shoved the buggy out of harm's way an instant before impact.

The word on the block is Bo just laughed, "Hell, one less bitch roaming the streets!" Cooder believes it's unlikely that part is true, or if it is, Bo must have thought he'd hit a female dog.

All Cooder knows is *he'd* be someone's bitch if not for Bo.

And all Bo ever wants for his trouble are cigarettes.

The thing about Bo is, he never knows when to shut up. He talks nonstop. About anything. Anything from the Australian sea floor four billion years ago to the best iced-brownie recipe in the world. An expert, at least in his own mind, about anything and everything.

What he never talks about is Bo Long. Cooder has a theory about that. Bo probably figured out a long time ago if he's an expert on everything, it leaves no time for anyone to ask him questions about himself.

Cooder once asked Bo if he ever wished things had turned out different for him—and the victim. "Every day, and hell, you see how much good it does either one of us."

Cooder shuffles toward the cafeteria sandwiched between two sweaty inmates.

◉ ◉ ◉

*Sunlight slants through golden sugar maples like an on-ramp to heaven. Cooder smiles. A balloon, yes, yes, an angel balloon tied to a mailbox gracefully bounces on the morning breeze.*

*"Hey, mister ... " A young girl's voice. "Please watch out, please pay attention ... "*

*Through a bloodshot haze, he sees blonde curls cascading from under a pink stocking cap and the small figure in a lavender cable-knit sweater and denim* jeans waves to him. Balanced on a shiny bicycle with sparkling white tires and a yellow bow attached at the handlebars, the girl peddles as fast as her young legs will allow.

"My mommy and daddy will be mad if they find out I'm riding my bike in the road. Please don't tell them, mister."

"No," he assures her, "I won't tell them. I'm not supposed to be driving, so we'll just keep each other's secret, okay?"

"Yeah, sure, okay. See ya!" she calls over her shoulder. Finally, she's a good distance up the driveway. Her smile reveals a quarter-moon dimple on each of her rosy cheeks. Safe. Unharmed.

◎ ◎ ◎

Cooder lurches forward. His shoulder slams into the concrete wall of the cafeteria.

"Coo Ward, what are you daydreaming about? You look like a zombie!" Bo's elbow digs into Cooder's ribs. "What the hell's the matter with you? Can't face another day of this swill and slop they call breakfast? Tell 'em this crap ain't fit for a dog! Hell, man, go ahead!"

Cooder grabs an empty food tray and shoves it hard into Bo's gut. "What the hell, Bo! Thought you'd skipped breakfast. Or did you just come down to *shove me* around?"

"Ooh-ooh, well, excuse me!" Bo backs off, waving his hands dramatically in mock surrender.

"Well, okay then." Cooder sets the tray down hard on the stainless rail that runs the length of the food line. Cooder will have no more trouble today separating truth from fiction or daydreaming things had turned out a whole lot different than they actually did. Bo had made sure of that, as usual.

## EIGHT

### IRISH – What an Angel Wants

When Gabe saw the sunflowers missing from the nightstand, I couldn't believe how he shot up in bed like flames inflating a hot air balloon.

I had to think quick, so I cracked the window and bellowed the sheer curtains hoping Gabe believed the wind had done the deed. Luckily, he spotted the sunflower remnants in the trashcan and crossed the room to lower the window.

None of that would have made sense to a clearheaded person. Yes, I know, Grandmother, old habits—like tidying up—die hard. And Gabe may not be so easily misled the next time.

If there *is* a next time, Grandmother would likely suggest I do something a little more understated, like she did after she passed during my senior year in high school. The day I was to give the graduation commencement speech in front of all my classmates and their parents, I was so paralyzed I couldn't even get dressed to leave the house. So, she removed the tiny pink rosebud earrings she'd left to me from my jewelry box and placed them on top of the lid. I'd been so surprised to see them there, but instinctively put them on. When I did, I felt her calm presence and knew I would kill that speech. And I did!

Fortunately, the sunflower incident is behind Gabe now as he pauses a few moments in the hallway at the sliver of daylight beneath the closed door to Leesie's room. He stares at his bare feet, shoves his hands into the front pockets of yesterday's jeans, and takes the stairs two treads at a time. In the distance, Destiny's nails clickity-click-click on the tile floor in the kitchen until the backdoor opens and closes.

After we lost Leesie, her bedroom door was a bone of contention for Gabe and me. Lord knows the number of times he'd walk down the hall to see the open door and proceed to shut it, forcefully. I'd come along and open it, sometimes even while he was still standing there. I admit for effect I twisted my wrist turning the doorknob and releasing it, letting the door swing open and bump lightly against the wall.

Sometimes I'd stand toe-to-toe with Gabe, though I barely came up to his shoulders, and remind him, "You can't keep Leesie's bedroom, or your emotions shut off from your life forever."

But he's still trying his best to do just that.

Gabe has only entered Leesie's room once in the last three years. That was two years ago today, on the first anniversary of Leesie's death and what would have been her tenth birthday.

He'd waited until I'd left the house that morning, then he'd gone into Leesie's room with an unopened whiskey bottle we kept for special occasions. If I had to guess, Gabe scanned Leesie's menagerie of stuffed animals including her favorite—an owl with a heart-shaped face. He might have opened one of her books; she had a book on everything from dinosaurs to *Charlotte's Web*. He likely paused in front of the poster of her all-time favorite movie, *The Wizard of Oz*, and the gallery of colorful crayon drawings taped to the wall, their edges yellowing and beginning to curl. He maybe touched some of the photographs of Leesie with Destiny, her friends and grandparents, her guncles, and us, the pictures stuck under the frame of the oval vanity mirror.

I arrived back home around noon that day and called to Gabe. I finally found him passed out, on his back, on Leesie's lavender flowered bedspread. One of the frilly pillow shams covered his face; the room reeked of stale liquor. I left him there.

Gabe wandered into the kitchen a couple of hours later, his torso in that question-mark silhouette he gets from lying on his back. I was struggling to open the back door, my hands full, holding a flower arrangement for Leesie's grave. We exchanged looks.

"Irish, where you going?" Gabe's face was the color of old celery. "Thought we were going to the cemetery together. I'll get my vest."

I heard his footsteps hit the stairs followed by the click of a closing door. Minutes later he reappeared with a noticeable bulge in one vest pocket. As we walked along the driveway toward the truck, Gabe fell behind, and soon there was a clank of the garbage can lid and glass striking glass. He sprinted ahead of me and unlocked the truck passenger door.

At the cemetery, I remember I couldn't stop shaking, my fingers running along the cold marble and the engraving: **Leesie Anne Hart, Our Butterfly, 10.01.01—10.01.10.**

Not a word or a touch had exchanged between us since the kitchen, but Gabe stood close behind me at our daughter's gravesite and steadied my shoulders. As we walked back to the truck, he interlaced his fingers with mine and raised my hand to his lips. I thought he was going to kiss my fingers, but instead he breathed warmth into my palm. We rode home in silence, his right hand on my left knee, only moving to shift gears.

We never spoke about that day, and Gabe never again opened the door or went into Leesie's room. It's as though he wants to remain closed off, like he has no strength left to find his way through life without Leesie and me. But he does. Oh, he does. If only Leesie's favorite character, Glinda the Good Witch from the *Wizard of Oz*, would wave her magic wand and remind Gabe, before it's too late, he's had "the power all along."

# NINE

## GABE – It Must Be Destiny

Destiny bounds out the kitchen door past Gabe and dives down the wooden steps to salute his favorite tree—favorite because it's the nearest.

Gabe pulls on his boots and jacket, and steps onto the back porch. He recalls the night before Leesie's sixth birthday. Irish, her long, buttery-blonde hair tossed over one shoulder in that way she had, slipped between the bedsheets, feet colder than usual, and snuggled extra close to him. He'd leaned in to kiss her, but she began chattering about an idea she had. They should get Leesie a dog for her birthday.

Gabe listened then cited reasons he was against the idea. He had an excellent argument, he thought, that their daughter's birthday was, after all, the very next day. There was no time to pull off something like Irish was suggesting. Gabe conceded that Leesie was mature enough to have a pet, so he suggested they think about a dog as a Christmas gift. "Only two months off," he pointed out and described how they could place the puppy in a large box, with air holes, topped with a giant red bow. "Probably early to mid-December we should start checking animal shelters." Irish threw him a quick smile and gave him three kisses before turning her back to him.

Good, Gabe had thought, we're in perfect agreement.

Less than seven hours later, with some ruse he'd since forgotten, Irish called upstairs for Gabe and Leesie to hurry and come to the back porch. When they did, they found a large white box with a gigantic red bow. Irish asked Leesie to hurry and lift the lid. She did, and a puppy with fur the color of beach sand hopped from the box and into Leesie's arms. Leesie was over the moon.

Gabe sighed, "Well, now how do you suppose?"

"Don't know, Gabe." Irish grinned up at him from where she knelt on the doormat tousling the pup's ears. "It must be destiny."

"Oh, Mommy!" Leesie had cried. "Is that his *name*? Oh, *Destiny*, you're going to live with us!"

The pup had jumped from Leesie's hug and scampered from one end of the back porch to the other, eluding his new family's calls and waving hands. Finally, the pup leapt onto Gabe's cold bare feet, its nails scratching like pieces of wire, and with a whimper, relieved itself, the tepid liquid seeping between Gabe's toes.

◉ ◉ ◉

Standing now in that memorable spot on the back porch, Gabe's grateful his toes are warm and dry. Out in the yard, Destiny runs through his daily routine, sniffing his way from his favorite tree to the overgrown shrubs against the utility garage.

Gabe takes the opportunity to inventory the spent dog food bags littering the back porch. He spots an empty coffee can on the white wicker settee and crouches among the crumpled bags on the floor to collect enough pellets for Destiny's breakfast. A fresh 20-pound bag of dog food waits in the truck bed, but Gabe has other plans for it later today.

"Hell-o-o!"

God. The last person he wants or needs to see this morning.

"Gabe? Good morning, son!"

Gabe acknowledges his relationship with his in-laws changed after Irish died. And he's the first to say his in-laws are the salt of the earth and will dare you to find better people anywhere than Willa and Evan Evans. And it isn't anything *they've* done that changed the relationship. It is just without Irish there, Gabe feels trapped with them living next door. They moved in after Jon and Sandy left, after the accident.

"I come bearing gifts!" Willa climbs the back porch steps, in one hand a picnic basket draped with a red-and-white checkered cloth napkin. Her hazel eyes stare intently at Gabe over the top of her speckle-framed, half-moon reading glasses. Her lips are set in a thin, straight smile, looking to Gabe like she believes she is his last—maybe *only*—hope of ever having another home-cooked meal.

Gabe's chest tightens. He sets the coffee can on the porch floor and stands slowly. Willa retreats down two steps and over to the right as Gabe moves across the porch floor. He pushes open the back screen door and moves back three paces. Willa advances up the two steps and onto the porch. Their movements are like a strangely choreographed tango between a very unlikely twosome.

Gabe has only danced with his mother-in-law once, at Irish's and his wedding reception. Willa led the whole time, like Irish had the first time he asked her to dance at high school homecoming. He and Irish had awkwardly dropped hands when the music ended but remained on the dance floor until the next song began. Irish relaxed in his arms that second dance and every other dance the rest of the night.

Willa, Gabe knows, rarely relaxes anywhere, so it is in that frazzled manner she enters the porch and moves toward Gabe. He holds the inside screen open with his back, standing almost at attention with his arms pressed to his sides, as Willa breezes by and into the kitchen. Gabe boots the dog food bags to the side of the porch and follows Willa inside.

Willa removes a Corningware dish from the basket and placed it on the counter and begins straightening the salt and pepper shakers and clearing dirty dishes from the kitchen table. Under her direction, a volcano of soap bubbles explodes in the porcelain sink, then the white plastic dish drainer on the counter disappears beneath water-beaded plates of varying sizes, an assortment of coffee cups, and drinking glasses ranging from juice to iced tea.

Gabe watches from across the room as Willa strategically places atop the dishes a saucepan. He's immediately transported to when Leesie as a toddler wore a pan on her head and beat out her own unique rhythm with a wooden spoon on the bottom of a plastic bowl.

"My *stars*, Gabe!" Willa's outburst snaps Gabe back to the moment. "It's *cold* in here. Did you order fuel oil?"

"You know, Willa," Gabe replies, shifting the conversation as he has no intention of pursuing the subject of fuel oil, "you don't have to do all that work every time you come over."

"Oh, land's sakes, Gabe, I know that!" She squirts Soft Scrub on a damp paper towel and wipes down the greasy stovetop. "Irish sure loved a clean kitchen though, didn't she? Guess we know who she got *that* from!"

Gabe shrugs and sits on a dinette chair on the far side of the table. For half a second he entertains asking if Irish visited Willa and Evan that morning. A crazy thought in more ways than one. If Irish had appeared to them, Willa would have run over in her nightgown shouting the news.

Instead, he asks, "Evan busy?"

"Oh, my," Willa begins, folding the spent paper towel tubing in half and stuffing it into the overflowing trashcan. "Tuesday morning Evan attended a Rotary meeting, or something like that, to give a prayer … "

Gabe zones out hearing Willa recount her clergyman husband's activities like she's his press secretary. Gabe nods occasionally from where he sits, but is more curious how juddery his legs are today. A nervous habit from childhood.

"Surely does him good to get out every day," she declares, her frosted bouffant disappearing in the refrigerator, checking the expiration dates on a milk carton and an unopened package of thick sliced bacon. "Think *you'll* feel like getting back to work soon, Gabe?"

And there it is. Not a visit goes by but what she doesn't ask that question. Sometimes she waits until she's out on the back porch step, staring back over her shoulder through the screen door. Regardless of the when, there is the inevitability she will ask the question.

Gabe had honestly intended to keep the balloon business going after they lost Leesie. But every time Tom urged Gabe to return calls from potential customers wanting to book flights, Gabe reasoned he didn't have the fortitude to pick up the phone, so he sure as hell wasn't ready to pilot a balloon.

He'd come up with every excuse in the book to avoid getting back to work. When the annual balloon and basket certification renewals arrived, he'd conveniently ignored them. Then Irish took ill. Gabe had cashed in his life insurance policy and used the proceeds for them to live on and pay medical bills. Irish shared her frustration with him, but ultimately had to focus on her health.

When Irish passed, Gabe knew he only needed money enough to hold Destiny and him for a year. Irish's life insurance payout had kept them afloat.

Ignoring Willa's question about work, Gabe notices as she busies herself in the kitchen that her back is a bit more bent than when they first met.

He guesses just like him, Willa and Evan have aged a bit over the last three years. And they are getting up there after all. He's glad there's leftover cash from Irish's policy he can leave them. He needs to remember to include in the note out in the van there is money in the gravy boat in the sideboard.

He watches Willa drop a damp paper towel onto the floor and move it under her shoe to rub out a dirty spot. Too bad she will never understand that all the cleaning and questions and home-cooked meals in the world will never persuade her son-in-law to live his life any differently that he is. And heaven forbid if Willa had a hint what he has planned for later today.

Willa picks up the paper towel and turns toward Gabe, still waiting for an answer to her question about work, but Destiny saves the day by scratching at the kitchen door.

Gabe isn't proud of the feeling, but it irkes him that when he lets Destiny in, the dog slides right past him and across the floor to Willa's feet, tail wagging like a hummingbird wing.

Gabe slaps his thigh to lure the dog. "Hey, boy! Looking for your breakfast?" He regrets the words the instant they leave his lips.

"Well now, where *is* his breakfast, Gabe? I swear he gets thinner every day. Of course, I could say the same for you. That reminds me … " Willa carefully removes an orange Tupperware bowl from her picnic basket.

"That other dish there on the counter has a special scrambled egg casserole with ground sausage and hash browns. You need to eat it before it gets cold. Oh, and don't let me forget to leave you biscuits. Now this here is vegetable beef soup with barley in it for lunch or dinner, or both. I'll set it in the refrigerator, but don't you forget about it, Gabe. Oh, doggone it. I didn't bring saltines. But I guess you have a full box since Irish was never *allowed* to eat … "

Gabe grabs the dog bowl off the floor and goes to the back porch, pulling the kitchen door closed behind him.

Did Willa think Gabe *wanted* to accept Irish's fate? Willa will go to her grave believing they should have more aggressively encouraged Irish to eat those last days. Even though Willa heard, just like he had, MJ say lack of appetite was a natural end-of-life progression. Irish's body no longer needed nourishment.

But Willa had begged, "Oh, Irish, sweetheart, just a few crackers." Did she think a cracker would keep her daughter alive a day or even an hour longer, so that some cure might be miraculously discovered and instantly administered?

Irish would gently whisper to Willa, "Mother, no more, please. It's what I want." But Willa would keep insisting and blaming Gabe because he listened to Irish's wishes.

Willa never knew Gabe kept a sleeve of unopened crackers in the nightstand, right next to Irish's side of the bed, just in case she ever changed her mind.

Gabe finds enough dog food from the bags on the porch to fill the bottom of the bowl then starts when he hears a sound like a soup ladle landing on the kitchen floor. Probably Willa's less than subtle way of getting his attention. Gabe returns to the kitchen to find Willa holding onto the oven handle so tightly it looks like her knuckles might pop right through her skin. On the counter next to the stove, he sees she'd removed from the cabinet a box of saltines, obviously a still too painful reminder of Irish's passing.

Gabe sets Destiny's bowl on the floor next to the water dish and debates whether to ask Willa if she's all right. It seems ridiculous not to, but it is, after all, Willa.

In Willa's world, she is the caretaker and champion over her domain. Try and offer help, and you have a major war on your hands. Gabe had no problem with that when Irish was alive because she knew how to handle her mother. But since her daughter's death, Willa is grieving by digging her boots in even deeper. Maybe Gabe relates too much to that strategy. All he knows is, whenever possible he avoids questioning Willa's commands or offering help.

Destiny nudges Willa's wrist with his nose, and she gently pats his muzzle. She lifts her head and pastes that familiar thin, straight smile on her face. "Gabe, I ... " her voice started slowly, but soon she sounded like her old self, "I should have thought to bring you some of those *oyscher* crackers you like so much ... ."

With that, Willa stuffs the checkered napkin into her picnic basket and bids Gabe goodbye with, "Good luck today, son."

Through the window above the sink, Gabe watches his mother-in-law's short, stout figure cut through the side yard, across the width of both their driveways, and into her and Evan's home, a house identical to his and Irish's.

He knows he should have been kinder to Willa this morning. He *knows* she means well. But he can't seem to help himself, he just keeps going out of his way to be indifferent to his in-laws, when he's not avoiding them altogether. Today, of all days, he should have been kinder to Willa.

The rich aroma of the fresh pot of coffee Willa brewed fills the kitchen while Gabe spoons a heaping portion of cheesy egg casserole onto a plate. He grabs two biscuits, one for him and one for Destiny, and heads for the table. Pausing again at the kitchen window, he looks out at the smoke pouring from his in-laws' chimney. "Neither of you deserves a sorry son-in-law."

# TEN

## IRISH – The Plan

I could kiss my mother! Now if Gabe had only let her pass through the kitchen into the rest of the house to clean it wall to wall, ceiling to carpet. No, of course, that's not going to happen today—or ever. And no, he didn't really *let* her into the kitchen. And yes, my mother is pushy and doesn't understand her limits when it comes to Gabe.

About the only thing they ever agreed on was to disagree with me about purchasing a mail-order house. Yes, put like that, buying a mail-order house sounds absurd. But The Castleton from Sears and Roebuck catalog is sturdy and the design flow surprisingly functional given it's a century old. The crazy thing is, as it turned out, my mother talked my dad into buying its twin, right next door. They learned our best friends were going to sell, so my parents made an offer on The Castleton II, as we called it, before it went on the market. My parents moved in exactly a year after Leesie died.

The day I first spotted the identical houses happened to be on Gabe's and my second-and-a-half anniversary.

"Oh, Gabe!" I waltzed into the apartment above the drugstore and across the kitchen linoleum like I was dancing with an invisible partner. "It's perfect! I don't know *how* I never noticed it before! Actually, there are two, but there's something special about the one."

Gabe was seated on a kitchen chair, still bundled in his jacket, unlacing his work boots. He straightened, and I plopped into his lap and hugged his neck. "Look, Irish," Gabe said, "I'm sorry, but I'm beat … "

I continued even though Gabe said he was exhausted. "530 Cedar Branch Lane. That's where it is. *The* house. Its twin stands right next door. Anyway, I don't usually go that way, but today, I don't know, the car kind of steered itself in that direction, and then I saw the house, and parked at the bottom of the drive and walked up to the front porch, which will be perfect for hanging ferns in the summer, and it already has a wooden swing, and I'm trying to remember how many steps up to the porch, but they're all in excellent condition, and the roof looks good, too, given the house must be close to a nundred years old, I would guess, but we can find out all that. Oh, did I mention it has two stories and four huge maples in the front yard? All three of us will be so happy there!"

Gabe brushed a lock of hair from my eyes.

I babbled on. "I knocked on the front door and called hello, but I guess no one was home. I can't wait to see the inside. I walked clear around the house. Looks like the bedrooms are upstairs. Nice screened porch on the back."

"Wait, Irish. Back up a minute. What do you mean the *three* of us?"

I jumped out of Gabe's lap and again danced around the kitchen, removing my coat in the process and throwing it in Gabe's direction. He caught it and placed it on the table without blinking an eye.

"That's what the doctor just confirmed, Mr. Gabriel 'Daddy' Hart. I know, the last time we said we'd wait, but nature—"

Irish, I'm putting in overtime at the water company so we can save to buy the balloon; you're working at the florist extra hours in hopes the Smiths retire in a year or two so you can take over … . Well, I mean, we'll make it work, with a baby and all, but not with buying a house."

Gabe put his hands on his knees and shook his head. I understood the financial commitment was a lot for him to take in. I also knew my husband didn't know how to express his *real* fear.

We'd celebrated in that kitchen before, twice over the last two years. Each time, within a week, he was sitting beside a hospital bed, drying my tears and reassuring me I'd done nothing wrong. That it just wasn't meant to be. That we were young, and there'd be plenty of time for us to have a family. We'd said we'd wait at least a couple of years, to get on our feet financially and give me plenty of time to heal—physically and emotionally.

I took a step toward him, unsure what to say next to help Gabe feel good about the baby, when he leapt to his feet.

"What am I *saying*? Really, Irish, you're … we're going to have … a baby?" He held me at arms' length and took in the whole of my body. Then he pulled me in and kissed every inch of my face. "Irish … Irish Cateline Evans Hart, I love you I love you I *love* you."

He moved to stand behind me and pressed against me; he placed his hands on my tummy. "So, little mother, how much do they want for this amazing house?"

I twirled around in his arms to face him. "Oh, Gabe, do you think the house is for *sale?*"

◎ ◎ ◎

Fast forward five years. Driving back to our cozy apartment with a Big Bird Birthday cake on the backseat, I acted on a whim and drove past *the* house of my dreams. I slammed on the brakes and the groceries, except for Leesie's cake, slid off the back seat onto the car floor. It was a stupid—reckless—reaction because the car behind me nearly didn't stop in time.

At the end of the driveway a woman wearing a gold blazer the color of autumn locust leaves pounded a "For Sale" sign into the ground.

Before the day was out, I was walking through the front door of the house. Once inside I was careful to stay a room away from the realtor while I phoned Gabe—I didn't want to appear overanxious to the agent. I knew Gabe and I would need to get the best possible deal if we were going to swing the sale financially. On the phone, I asked Gabe if he agreed what I described would be a perfect place for a downstairs powder room. "There's a closet off the kitchen," I whispered. "You and Jon could easily turn it into a half-bath. Water's right there. And just enough room for a commode and pretty little standalone basin. I can't *believe* the owners hadn't made that a priority." Gabe asked how in the world he could know without seeing it.

So, the next day I returned to the house with Gabe. He spotted trouble areas—the furnace was old and a lot of the electric would need rewiring. All logical reasons to walk away, but there was no way I was backing down. And actually, Gabe agreed the house had a certain kind of charm to it. And, yes, the kitchen closet could be repurposed into a powder room.

But with a mortgage and high interest rates, he warned me that we'd both be hobbling around on canes before the house was paid for. And resale? He doubted we'd get out of it what we put in. And there was the winding two-lane road with that funky curve at the end of the driveway. I never told him or Mother about the wreck I'd nearly caused the day the house went up for sale.

Mostly my mother had been dumbfounded to think that anyone would order a house from a catalog. And why in the world would a young couple a century later buy it when there were newer homes to choose from? Mother spent hours researching the house's history, with my brother offering his computer skills to feed her information.

"Irish, I know you think that house is adorable and have already mentally hung ferns on the front porch." Mother had marched into our apartment and plopped a thick folder on the kitchen table. "And lord knows it's got a great history. But, honey, those stairs, that furnace, and the work to put in the half bath. And that *driveway!* Right on that horrible curve."

I would hear none of it. Finally, Mother shrugged her shoulders. My dad? He just wanted his baby girl to be happy.

Gabe has yet to forgive any of us for the decision.

And now my mother has forgotten to do something very important for me when she was in the kitchen this morning. She was *supposed* to change the wall calendar to the next month, like she's done the first day of every other month all year.

Yes, my mother has been my accomplice since a few weeks before I passed. The calendar and having her turn the page each month was one of three things I prearranged before I died, to help Gabe today, when he finds himself at a crossroads, which I greatly fear he has.

Turning the page of a calendar is minor compared to my ultimate plan that Gabe see Cooder Ward in prison on this date—something I've believed since I first visited the prison is necessary for Gabe to move past the death of our daughter.

Gabe is such a good man; he would never knowingly break a promise to me. That's why I framed my plan as a promise—giving me his word he would see Cooder Ward. My hope is when Gabe sits across from the man who killed our daughter, Gabe will no longer feel the hate and rage he is carrying with him every day. I pray he instead feels forgiveness—like I did.

The third plan I devised for today is, well, a bit of a ruse. Gabe will question all day long my reasoning behind a chore I have scheduled for him this morning—taking Destiny for his annual vet visit.

The thing is this, when Destiny came into our lives, though he was a gift for Leesie, he quickly gave Gabe a way to deal with relationship issues he'd wrestled with from growing up in foster care. I knew, of course, about Snoopy, the dog Gabe had secretly named, fed, and cared for. The way Gabe tenderly described Snoopy, the dog had clearly been something special, something the young boy allowed himself to love and receive love from, unconditionally, when he didn't feel safe to love or be loved by anyone else.

As an adult, it took a little time for Gabe to trust how he felt about me. Oh, but the *second* Leesie was born, he was head over heels in love with our little girl. Then Dest came along, and I saw a tenderness well up in Gabe that again he couldn't help but express. I think for Gabe, he can't *help* how he feels about Leesie and me, and Destiny, but is still guarded when it comes to allowing himself to express or receive love from anyone else.

So, knowing the bond between Gabe and Destiny, and that our dog might be the only *living* thing Gabe would be able to connect with, I contrived a plan before I died where Gabe would *have* to closely interact with

Destiny and acknowledge feelings of empathy and compassion before he faces Cooder Ward.

I'm only here for a short time today. But I know for Gabe, today is not the day for him to leave this world, though he thinks it is, and thinks he *wants* it to be.

I think, I believe, I hope, the love he feels for and from Destiny will help determine Gabe's destiny.

# ELEVEN

## GABE – Choices

Elbows on the table, Gabe pokes fork tines at the food on his breakfast plate. He manages a third small bite, then stands and scrapes the cold biscuit and remaining egg casserole into the kitchen garbage can.

Maybe the next owners will install a garbage disposal, he thinks, and update the cabinets and appliances, and finally turn that kitchen closet into a half bath—a winter project he and Irish had slated three years ago. They lost Leesie, and he hasn't done crap.

He sets his plate and fork in the sink and runs water over both. He thinks about adding dish liquid, but he's seen firsthand how after loss his mother-in-law craves busy work—and busy work she'll need today after learning of the loss of her son-in-law.

He turns toward the dining room, and out of the corner of his eye notices the colorful calendar Willa hung on the wall back in January. At the time, she said she got it because each month had a picture of a different special shape hot air balloon. He always assumed the calendar was a ploy to get him back to work.

Gabe crosses the kitchen to take a closer look at September's featured special shape, the Harley Davidson balloon. He doesn't need to read the caption beneath the photograph; Gabe knows the balloon's history, how Malcolm Forbes's crazy passion for motorcycles led him to commission the special shape. Gabe can only imagine how many hours it takes to set up, inflate, and pack up that sucker.

Wanting a closer look, he removes the calendar from the wall and studies the picture. He's flown in the Albuquerque Fiesta many times so he recognizes the Sandia Mountains in the background of the Harley photograph. His plan three years ago was to take the family to the next balloon fest in Albuquerque, that was if Leesie had as much fun as he thought she would on her first flight with him. Of course, the Albuquerque trip never happened.

Curious what special shape balloon is highlighted for the month of October, he flips the calendar page.

Gabe grabs the back of the nearest chair to steady himself. What the hell? In red marker on the first day of October is an appointment reminder, in Irish's handwriting.

*Destiny — Vet Annual @ 10 am*

When did *Irish* write on the calendar? He thumbs through the two remaining months, then all previous months. No writing on any of the other pages.

Could Irish have scribbled the reminder this morning? Is it another—or maybe a real sign she was here?

Stop it. Just *stop* it. There's a logical explanation. Has to be. Irish and Willa must have cooked up the whole thing before Irish passed. Willa would have been her daughter's more-than-willing coconspirator—from hanging the calendar in January to changing it out every month. Until a minute ago, Gabe can't remember ever glancing at the calendar after Willa drove the nail in the wall, but apparently she's been changing it each month since January, except for today, September to October.

He's not surprised she forgot this morning during her visit. She was visibly overwrought when she saw the box of crackers—a too painful reminder of her inability to save her daughter those final days.

Gabe begins to try and get into Irish's ever-clever mind about the appointment. He imagines that if Willa's visit had gone as planned, she'd have likely strolled over to the calendar, changed the month, and said something like, "Oh, look. Destiny has a vet visit today!"

Based on how Irish would have imagined Gabe's reaction to seeing the appointment in her handwriting, Willa was probably instructed to tell Gabe that her daughter just wanted to make sure Destiny stayed current on his shots. So, she'd simply commissioned Willa to find the perfect 12-month calendar and a red marker for Irish to write the reminder, hang the calendar in January, and change it out the first day of every month. And, to lighten the shock of it all for Gabe if it had gone as planned, Willa might have added one of her classic phrases, "Easy-peasy!"

Gabe shakes his head. Why in heaven's name would Irish schedule Destiny's vet visit for October 1? Obviously she knew the *significance* of the date—the anniversary of Leesie's birth and death. Not to mention October 1 is the day he's promised to make a prison visit—because *she'd* insisted he promise to do so on that date! So, Irish, why didn't you have *that* on the calendar?

Well, technically, until her last breath, Irish hadn't known for sure he would visit the prison on October 1. He hadn't yet promised her.

Gabe isn't sure if he is more upset with Irish for concocting the plan or with Willa for orchestrating the scheme. Either way, the vet visit adds a major hitch in the day's schedule.

He looks again at the appointment reminder. Hold on. Just because there was an appointment today, doesn't mean he has to *keep* it.

Grabbing his phone from a jeans pocket to call the vet's office, he's hit with yet another revelation.

Gabe's plan has been to drop Destiny at Irish's brother's house around noon, under the pretense that The Castleton wouldn't have heat until the next day so could the dog stay overnight with Michael and Scot. No, he'd tell them, he'll be fine to stay in the house. He'll just bundle up because he needs to stick around for the oil delivery early the next morning. Gabe's real intent, of course, was to leave Destiny permanently with them.

Michael and Scot have a big fenced-in backyard, one of the reasons they bought the house a few months ago. They aren't completely settled in yet, but have mentioned to Willa, who couldn't wait to tell Gabe during one of her morning visits, they are anxious to adopt a dog.

Knowing that Michael and Scot look forward to having a pet in the near future, and how much they loved Destiny, and Destiny adores them, they seemed like the perfect choice to care for Destiny going forward.

But now Gabe is just remembering Irish mentioned a couple of times that Dr. Mac and his wife foster dogs, when the right opportunity comes along. Gabe knows Destiny loves seeing Dr. Mac, jumping in the truck at the mention of his name. So, maybe Gabe can leave Destiny with Dr. Mac, instead of Michael and Scot. The guys could adopt a rescue puppy when *they* were ready.

He looks again at the reminder on the calendar. Irish's micromanaging might have actually helped him today after all. Time he'll now have to spend at the vet's office is time he won't have to spend dropping Destiny off at Michael's.

# TWELVE

## COODER – The First Visit

The speaker embedded in the infirmary window crackles. "What, no comment?"

Puzzled, Cooder stares through the double security glass at the guard with the smirk, who is manning the microphone.

Cooder rubs the back of his neck. Now he remembers. As inhibited as Cooder is most of the time, he prides himself on a pretty fair sense of humor. During his second visit to the prison infirmary, it had entered his mind to say, "No change in my insurance since the last visit," as if he were just showing up at a doctor's office on the outside. The guard had broken into a half smile and hadn't yelled at him, so Cooder's continued the joke during subsequent appointments.

"No, sir. None today," Cooder answers.

The guard shrugs and buzzes Cooder into the small windowless waiting room. As happens on each of his visits when he sees the three empty gray metal chairs are arranged haphazardly, he places them along the wall an equal distance apart. Today, when he finally takes a seat, he studies the wall clock protected behind a wire mesh. The red second hand makes quick, short movements around the stark white clock face. 7:45. And counting, he adds to the thought.

He's reminded of the clock in the prison visitor area and Irish's first visit.

He'd been startled when a guard outside his cell said, "Cooder Ward, a woman here to see you." He'd wondered why in the world Charlene would show up mid-week. He'd hoped nothing was wrong.

When he walked through the visitor area door and saw the woman was not his wife, he'd wished it had been her, even if Charlene had come to deliver the worst news in the world. Yes, the woman was on Cooder's list of approved visitors, he just never thought he'd ever see her there.

The guard pushed Cooder toward the chair across from young woman. He'd been relieved to see through the glass that her eyes were lowered. She wore a light green top and sat perfectly still and straight in her metal chair. Her hair was pulled away from her face, up in a headband of some sort, and her purse rested square on the shelf in front of her, her hands folded on top of it. Cooder remembered thinking she looked kind of prim and proper sitting there, but he thought most likely she was anxious. He knew how uneasy a person—he imagined especially so a visitor—could feel with armed officers watching every move.

They'd sat opposite each other an awful long time, her eyes fixed on her purse and his focused on her out of the respect he knew he owed her. It hadn't taken him a split-second to glance up at the visitor area wall clock, but when he looked back through the security glass, her eyes were waiting to lock onto his.

She immediately reached for the black phone hanging to her right. She lifted the receiver off the cradle, held it to her ear, and waited for Cooder to do the same.

He'd just sat there, his right arm paralyzed. Irish turned her eyes toward his phone and back again to him. It was as if a puppeteer had tied strings to his arm, the way his hand floated toward the receiver, grabbed it, and placed it at his ear.

"Mr. Ward." Her voice was soft but not timid, and for a moment eased the pounding of his heart. "I'm Irish Hart."

"I … yes, ma'am."

Prior to that day he'd heard her speak a few times during the trial. But hearing her voice through the phone, her words right there in his ear, and watching her lips move only a few feet away was painfully different than in the courtroom. Painfully personal.

"Mr. Ward … I didn't come here to make you feel any worse than I imagine you already do. And I certainly didn't come to moralize or preach."

"No, ma'am."

Cooder knew her dad was a preacher, but never imagined she'd be the kind to sermonize. Still, he didn't know why she'd come, or *what* she was going say. Whatever terrible thing she might utter, he knew he deserved it—and worse.

"Mr. Ward," she began again, having paused to take in slow, deep breaths, probably to calm the quiver in her voice. "I wondered, and yes, I know it wouldn't be normal, whatever normal means, and, of course, it would only be if you're agreeable, but, well, I wondered if it would be possible … " She paused again, this time as though upset with herself that she'd begun to just blurt things out. She straightened her back and lifted her chin. "I wondered, Mr. Ward, if it would be possible for us to … to become friends."

Cooder's shoulders collapsed, his chest caved, and bile filled his throat. Irish had said what she'd come to say, and she was waiting for Cooder's response.

What could he say to her request? God knew Cooder Ward didn't deserve such kindness. He needed to say *something* but feared opening his mouth because his lunch was getting harder to choke back. Fortunately, what came spilling from his lips weren't franks and beans.

"Oh, Missus Hart, if only I could go back and change everything, please know I would … I'm so … I know words aren't enough, oh, but I'm so, so sorry. I want to apologize to you, to you and Mr. Hart—"

"Yes, I know. I truly believe you are sorry." She lowered her eyes and watched her fingers run along her purse handle. "We got your letter."

"Yes, ma'am." He'd hoped they had. He'd never expected them to write him back. He never really wanted them to. He wondered if the letter might be in her purse.

"Mr. Ward, if you'll bear with me. I don't exactly know how to do this under the circumstances. But, well … " She looked up at Cooder, this time with misty blue eyes. "If it's alright with you, I'd like to come back this Sunday for a visit. But not if it'll cut short time you could have with your family."

"No, that would be fine. Charlene, that's my wife, she'd be fine with it. Sometimes she can't get off work … . Yes, Missus … "

"Maybe you could call me Irish?"

"Okay, Missus … " A guard poked Cooder's shoulder indicating time was up. "And, well, if you want, but you don't have to, I mean, if you want to, I'm just plain Cooder."

"Well then, Cooder ... See you Sunday."

She hung up the phone receiver, stood and walked halfway to the door before Cooder managed "Yeah, see ya ... Missus Hart."

◎ ◎ ◎

"Ward! Maybe you need your *ears* examined instead of your damn eyes. Get over here."

Cooder leaps from the infirmary waiting room chair and apologizes to the guard before he remembers Bo's words. "Never tell the sons of bitches you're sorry."

# THIRTEEN

## IRISH – The First Visit

On my first trip to visit Cooder Ward, I turned the car around halfway there and drove back home. When I'd left the house earlier that morning, I'd tossed my handbag on the back porch settee while I struggled to get my keys out of the backdoor lock. The handbag, with my driver's license, had remained on the settee cushion.

An hour later than I'd originally planned, but fortunately with my handbag, I arrived at the prison parking lot where I proceeded to step out of the car into a rogue cloudburst. I darted toward the entrance marked *Visitors* using my handbag like an umbrella, but my hair got drenched, and my skirt clung to my legs, and I came this close to saying the hell with it. But I'd come too far.

I wiped the soles of my sandals on the commercial-grade entry rug, but still slipped when I stepped onto the floor of the visitor center. An imposing guard with crooked eyeglasses reached out to steady me. I withdrew my arm, and he stepped back, planting his shiny black boots on the dull concrete floor, his right hand resting on his sidearm.

Knowing I had to produce picture ID, I rummaged in my bag for the wallet holder that contained my driver's license. My license was stuck to the plastic see-through window, and when I tried to get it unstuck, the holder flew out of my hand and into the air. The bespectacled guard caught it with his right hand and presented it to me.

"May I help you?" He enunciated each word with equal tonal quality and spacing, like Robocop, with not even a slight rise on "you" to indicate he was asking a question. He cleared his throat, and I watched how he methodically extended his index finger to push his eyeglasses up and over a hump on his nose. I quickly lowered my gaze because the lens magnified the size of his eyes in an eerie way. I wondered if he got that a lot, people averting their eyes because his were buggy behind the thick glass. I remember thinking if he'd had eye disease as a child, he'd surely suffered from getting bullied.

Between forgetting my driver's license, driving back to get it, getting rain soaked, slipping on the floor, and then flipping my license into the air—not to mention feeling dreadful for my rudeness to the guard, I was a wreck. Then I took in the visitor welcome center's high security glass enclosures, barred doors, and warning signs, none of which evoked *any* feeling of being welcoming. I lifted my chin in hopes I could force the tears to stay in my eyes.

"Ma'am, are you ... "

The guard was mid-sentence when I spun on my heel and ran out of the windowless building into unexpected blinding sunlight. Before I could shield my eyes, I bumped into a woman digging in her purse. "Excuse me,"

I mumbled, dashing to the car. I threw my handbag in the backseat, started the engine, and sobbed into a flimsy napkin I pulled from the glove box.

Days afterwards I mentally replayed the scene with the guard. I'd missed something; I just knew it. I came to realize I'd projected my fears onto an officer who meant *me* no harm. When he'd adjusted his glasses, his enlarged hazel eyes were soft around the edges. And when he'd spoken a second time, his voice was emotive; he seemed genuinely concerned about me.

Still, even though I'd reconciled my first experience, I might never have gone back to the prison a second time if I hadn't a few days later noticed a spray of plastic flowers stuck into the ground *behind* Leesie's headstone. It was August, the year after Leesie died, so I couldn't be sure how long the spray had been there; intense summer sun could quickly fade most anything.

I thought it strange the flowers were in back of the headstone. I even wondered if they'd been intended for another gravesite. Regardless, I wasn't thrilled with the small, cheap arrangement compared to the professional bouquets, the huge hydrangeas, and real yellow rose buds I brought from the flower shop every few days. When I left the cemetery that day, I tossed the fake roses in a trashcan near the parking lot, along with the wilted flowers I'd replaced with big, colorful, fresh blossoms.

The following week when I pulled into the cemetery parking lot, which was generally empty on a Wednesday morning unless they had a service, I saw a car in the last space and a redheaded woman a distance away. I parked my car and went around to retrieve a bouquet from the passenger floorboard.

As I neared Leesie's grave, I stepped behind a tree upon seeing a woman paused at the back of my daughter's headstone. She knelt and ran her hand along the ground where the plastic flowers had been, as though to confirm the spray was no longer there. She raised her head and scanned the neighboring gravestones. I assumed she was looking to see if possibly the spray had been moved to another grave.

The woman, who I guessed to be about my age, collapsed to the ground on one hip, her hand on the back of Leesie's tombstone. Oh, my stars, I thought. Of course. I recognized the flaming red hair. The woman's shoulders trembled; I understood the meaning of trembling shoulders. Charlene Ward was crying. She didn't remain long before she hurried with lowered eyes to her car.

I followed her to the parking lot and introduced myself. It was a brief meeting, but there was a connection that can only be felt by two people who have together suffered loss. An unspeakable sorrow that truly needs no words. Words cannot convey the depth of grief one feels at a death of a child. What passes between those two people is hallowed and sacred.

I knew at that moment I had to return to the prison. Charlene Ward, who every day of the trial sat in the gallery right behind her husband, was a reminder that Leesie's death affected more than a little girl's family.

I realized, too, the first time I'd gone to the prison, I'd gone there because my heart was broken into pieces, and the gaping open wounds were riddled with unbearable sorrow, and my life with Gabe was decomposing before my eyes while I helplessly watched hatred fester and spread inside him.

I also now believe the first visit hadn't panned out because I'd gone for the wrong reason. I'd gone to see Cooder Ward to spite Gabe. To show him I was better than he was. God, I hate admitting that even *now*.

I'd ignored what the visit itself would involve, only how I would hold my great act of courage over Gabe's head. I would tout how high and mighty I was; *Irish Hart* visited the man who killed their daughter.

But Charlene Ward's visit to Leesie's grave, her genuine remorse for the loss of a little girl's life, and an unpretentious spray of flowers placed in a discreet spot behind the headstone had humbled me. What had I been thinking? We were *all* grieving Leesie's death. I was burying my grief with a self-righteous attitude while Charlene Ward exposed her heart and soul out of respect for the dead.

The scar around my heart was ugly, and I wept and prayed to be shown compassion until I was ready to forgive.

All that said, Cooder Ward would not have been ready for a visit from me that first time. Because when I sat across from him the next week, he looked like he'd rather the devil himself had come to claim his soul. I still hadn't decided what I'd come to say, but I knew if I kept picturing Charlene Ward's trembling shoulders, then the right and decent thing would come to me. When I uttered the words, questioning if Cooder Ward and I could possibly be friends, I was as shocked as he appeared to be.

Today I fear that if my husband doesn't face our daughter's killer, hatred will eat him from the inside out until there is nothing left of Gabriel George Hart. He doesn't have to become Cooder Ward's *friend*. He just has to face him.

The last time I saw Cooder Ward, we dodged the subject that we would never see each other again. We both knew I was growing too weak to drive myself to the prison any longer. We didn't say goodbye—what could we have said? I left the prison that afternoon with my heart set on Gabe visiting Cooder Ward after I passed, maybe on Leesie's birthday. My intent was not to further punish either Gabe or the man responsible for

Leesie's death. I believed then, and still do, they both need to face each other and their demons.

Yes, I still believe that. But today I've come to realize Gabe visiting Cooder Ward may not be all that is needed to avert him from self-destruction.

# FOURTEEN

## GABE – Yellow Butterfly Pajamas

Gabe watched from the living room window as the amber warning lights flashed and the octagonal red sign extended at a 90-degree angle from the county school bus. The yellow paint looked bright and shiny as the bus came to a halt at the end of the driveway. Intense crimson brake lights illuminated on vehicles that had moments before sent fallen leaves swirling.

As was his ritual every school morning, Gabe mentally willed all drivers to stop their vehicles, to obey the law for the safety of the young lives already riding bus number eight, and those about to board. Across the street, first-grader Sherry Leigh let go of her mother's hand, looked to her right, and left, walked in front of the stopped traffic and the bus, took hold of the handrail, and climbed safely inside the Big Bird-colored chariot. The bus disappeared around the curve and drivers went on their way.

Gabe had nearly missed the bus this morning given the time it had taken for him to process the newly discovered vet appointment. When he did realize it was time for the bus, he overshot throwing the calendar onto the kitchen table. He left it where it landed on the floor and marched to the front living room window. As a rule, Gabe was in position long before the bus arrived. Now, another part of his routine out of synch this morning, was further indication how challenging the day promised to be.

"Gabe, you're obsessed." Irish would chant at eight o'clock every school morning. "Staring out that window motionless as the mailbox at the end of the driveway."

She'd come up beside him, her hands on her hips, shaking her head. The first few times he said flat out there was no harm in him looking out the living room window for a few minutes, or an hour, or all day long if he wanted to, which he wasn't sure but what he might have done.

Finally, Irish asked him one day, "Do you think watching the school bus every morning helps keep students like little Sherry safe? Leesie's accident had nothing to do with the bus. Still, do you think it will somehow bring Leesie back?"

Gabe had known he was going too far when he answered, but said it anyway, "Irish, I *know* it wasn't the bus! And do you seriously think I believe I can alter history by *wishing* I'd been at the end of the driveway that day, instead of catching a quick shower before *you* started filling the damn washer with hot water?"

A few weeks later, he noticed Irish made additional comments during the course of the day, over the dinner table or while riding in the truck to the cemetery. She was less adamant with those remarks and did qualify each as "only a suggestion," but their frequency sent a clear message: he wasn't moving through his grief of losing Leesie fast enough.

Like Willa, Irish would bring up the subject of Gabe getting back to work. And, yes, they were "only suggestions," but Gabe had made it clear he was not ready to take the balloon out or fly paid balloon passengers, and he wasn't going to call Tom, and definitely not Jon. And he didn't want to drive chase or crew for any of his balloon buddies, though they had called numerous times to invite him. And he had no intention of attending balloon association meetings or running for treasurer or editing that ridiculous newsletter.

He knew then he should have shared with Irish how proud he was of her for reopening the florist shop a month after the accident. He guessed getting back into a regular routine and hearing the ding of the little bell above the door signaling a customer's arrival had been healing for her. Irish loved to help brighten customers' days with fresh flowers.

That early morning routine he and Irish had established at the window continued until the day the sky was an eerie steel gray and it appeared to him no life stirred outside, not a bird in sight. It was then he noticed instead of hearing Irish nag him at the living room window, he heard her murmuring in the dining room on the other side of the French doors that stood slightly ajar.

In spite of the eeriness of the morning, the bus completed its school day routine after which Gabe abandoned his post. He crossed the living room and peered through the small gap between the two dining room doors.

Irish stood at the end of the dining room table nearest the doors, with her back to Gabe. Five of the ladder-backed chairs that he would have expected to be spaced equally around the table were instead arranged in a line against the wall at far end of the room. The sixth chair was to Irish's left.

Standing there he reflected on the times Irish would quip that Gabe could get dressed in a fresh flannel shirt and new jeans, and before he left the bedroom, both were faded and frayed. That was an exaggeration, of course; well, sort of.

On the other hand, as her brother commented when he helped them move from the apartment to The Castleton, Irish had clothes from high school she wore regularly, but they always appeared to be brand new. And when Michael spoke at Irish's memorial service, he shared that during the aftermath of the accident and the course of the trial, any time he felt overcome with grief, all he needed do was look at his sister. "How put together she always was, her hair pulled up in that way she had that probably took a lot of time but appeared effortless, her sweater without a single pill or a wrinkle in her skirt." He said Irish's style and grace had given him faith that they'd all somehow survive the whole awful mess of losing Leesie.

That was the Irish Gabe had expected to greet him that eerie morning. But the Irish he saw in the dining room had hair tousled like she'd been standing in front of an inflator fan filling a hot air balloon. Her robe hung off one shoulder with wadded-up Kleenexes overflowing the pockets and its tie-belt dangling long and limp from one loop.

Strewn in front of Irish on the rectangle table were paper patterns, a tangled cloth tape measure, and spools of thread, one of which was rolling across the tabletop. On the chair next to her rested a large wicker basket filled with brightly colored garments.

Gabe initially thought Irish was making a dress for herself. He'd overheard her telling Willa a day or two before how she bet her dad would love to see her wearing something bright and cheerful on Easter so that when he looked for his daughter from the pulpit, as he always did, he would think of yellow daffodils or red tulips.

But of course, that made no sense. The summer Leesie was two, Irish swore off sewing after her failed attempt to make their daughter a simple one-piece sundress. About an hour into its one and only wearing, two buttons fell off and a side seam split. Gabe helped Irish return the sewing machine to its rightful owner. She thanked her mother and apologized. "Your Singer, I couldn't get it to carry a tune!"

Irish shifted her position at the dining room table, and Gabe saw the notorious Singer sewing machine. He was trying to mentally connect the dots when with her right hand Irish picked up a pair of cutting shears and reached her other hand into the wicker basket and pulled out Leesie's white christening gown.

"*Irish!*" Gabe pushed open the French doors. He got to Irish as the scissor blades sliced into their daughter's baptismal dress. "What the hell are you doing?" He grabbed her shoulders and spun her until she faced him.

"What the hell am *I* doing? What the hell are *you* doing, Gabe? You nearly made me cut off my finger!" She waved the scissors and pieces of the lacy white material in front of her. As she did, he'd flashed back to when Irish's hands cradled little Leesie in that white dress and holy water was sprinkled from a yellow rosebud, and how droplets dotted their daughter's tiny, pink forehead.

"What am I doing? What am *I* doing?" He snatched the material from Irish's hand. "Irish, this is what Leesie was *baptized* in! What's wrong with you?"

"Wrong with *me*? Ah! This coming from a man who curses God under his every breath?" Irish faced the table and reached into the wicker basket, her hands visibly shaking. She grabbed a turquoise T-shirt and jammed material between yawning scissor blades.

"Irish, don't. Please." Gabe touched Irish's chin with unsteady fingers. She resisted at first, but finally he eased her around to again face him. Her arms fell lifeless at her sides and her eyes lowered, tears trailing down her cheeks, dampening his fingertips. He whispered, "Is this what you really want?"

"No! ... No, of course not. What I *really* want ... " Irish paused with a deep sigh, her eyes level with where his half-buttoned flannel shirt fell open at his chest. "What I *really* want ... is to have *Leesie* back." Eyes like pools of blue water looked up at him. "But, I know she's gone ... We can't ever have her back. I just thought something, maybe a quilt, something soft to hold ... to wrap ourselves up in ... to *hide* under for all I know ... " Her voice had been steadily rising as she spoke. Then it fell out in a hushed tone. "Well, I just thought maybe it could make the pain ... a little easier on us both."

He'd heard her, but the more Gabe studied the swatch of Leesie's christening gown he held in his hand, the more outraged he became. He pulled away from Irish. "I will never—*ever*—so much as ... so much as *look* at that quilt, Irish!" He slammed the remnant on the table and went back to his place at the living room window.

Moments of deafening silence were broken by the sound of working scissors. He glanced over his shoulder to see Irish cut off the sleeves of Leesie's yellow butterfly pajamas—the ones she wore the morning Destiny arrived on their doorstep.

As if on cue, Dest slinked through the kitchen door into the dining room, tail between his legs. He stood for a time, his coal black eyes looking back and forth from Gabe in the living room to Irish in the dining room. Finally, the dog moved toward Irish and brushed her robe with his body. She didn't acknowledge him, but he stayed close at her feet, his nose level with the edge of the table, inches from the cottony yellow fabric.

Gabe turned and stared blankly out the window. He believed Destiny recognized the significance of Leesie's pajamas. Apparently even the dog remembered those pjs and maybe even how warm Leesie's hugs must have been that first morning. How could Irish so selfishly destroy irreplaceable memories?

The continuous sound of scissors snipping Leesie's clothes into pieces maddened Gabe like water dripping incessantly from a faucet in the middle of the night. Snip—Irish's actions were inhuman. Snip—She was heartless. Snip—And for what, a *quilt?*

Gabe marched to the dining room doorway, and the cutting stopped. Irish turned, tears streaming down her face. Gabe opened his arms wide. She leaned forward, slightly, toward him. He grabbed the door handles on either side of him, stepped backward and pulled the French doors closed with such force that a windowpane fell out and shattered into pieces when it hit the floor.

# FIFTEEN

## JON – When Innocence Ruled

Jon Elam stops his blue Volvo short of the security gate and leans forward to gaze through the windshield at the not one, but two rolls of razor concertina wire atop the massive chain-link fence. Three taps on the driver window glass startle him. He lowers the window with an apology and surrenders his driver's license to an armed guard. The guard thumbs through papers secured to a clipboard while Jon rubs his jacket cuff on the steering wheel to dry moisture left by his clammy palms.

Jon follows the guard's directions to an area of the parking garage marked physicians only. He pulls into an open space at the head of the row and cracks the door to check the car's alignment between the white lines. He readjusts the position of the car, backing up and pulling in again. He turns off the engine and removes his cell from an inside jacket pocket. 8:00 AM. He's late. Jon opens the driver door quickly to bright sunlight streaming at an angle into the garage and a shadow of a man standing by the car.

"Good morning, Dr. Elam."

Jon climbs out of the car to the extended hand of the prison warden. The warden's grip is firm and his handshake vigorous enough to cause Jon's shoulder to move up and down. It's a handshake a person doesn't forget and one he's already experienced at Chris Proffitt's holiday party. "Good morning, Warden."

"As you see, I'm on my way out." Jon glances past the warden at the Mercedes 500SL idling close by with the driver door ajar. "But I wanted to welcome you personally and thank you for covering for Dr. Proffitt. On un-*usually* short notice."

The warden studies Jon's face. "You appreciate, I'm sure, a strict regimen is the cornerstone of our correctional facility. Dr. Proffitt assured me that you, too, are a stickler for protocol. As a *professional* in the field of medicine…"

A ringtone interrupts him, and the warden removes his cell from his coat pocket and checks caller ID. "I have to take this."

When Jon offers his hand to bid goodbye, the warden steps forward and plants his free hand squarely on Jon's shoulder. "I've alerted my staff to *closely* monitor the prisoner's examination and escort you to my captain's office in the event there are *any* issues." The warden turns and marches toward his car, barking orders into his cell.

Jon considers the light gray Mercedes exiting the garage. It wasn't just *what* the warden said, but the manner in which he did so. And what was with the hand on the shoulder? Clearly Jon was expected to get the message—don't *try* anything.

The warden, of course, had been the one to authorize Jon to examine Cooder Ward in Chris Proffitt's absence. Jon's close friend, Chris, was Cooder Ward's eye surgeon, and given the connection between the replacement doctor and Cooder Ward, Jon understood approval was met with pushback.

During his call to the warden, Chris had vouched for his colleague's personal and professional integrity, level-headedness, and medical expertise. He assured the warden that Elam was the only eye doctor Chris would want to perform surgery on him or anyone in his family. The warden's final argument had been security clearance would be impossible given the short notice. Chris had respectfully reminded the warden that Elam had remotely coordinated the Ward case and the prisoner's care since day one and subsequently he already *had* clearance. The warden finally put Chris on speakerphone as he ordered his captain to beef up security for Elam's examination of the prisoner.

Jon had later asked Chris what swayed the warden's decision; was it because Jon already had clearance? Chris said, if he had to guess, it was when Chris asked the warden one question. "Don't we owe it to Dr. Elam, considering who donated the corneas used for Cooder Ward's transplant?"

Jon's cellphone vibrates, and Chris Proffitt's name appears. For a split-second Jon hoped it was Gabe calling. Until three years ago, they talked multiple times a day. But his best friend hadn't spoken to Jon since the accident. And if Jon ever needed to talk to Gabe, it's now. After the examination, Jon decides, he'll try again to reach out to Gabe. Though he's sure his effort will have the same end result his hundreds of previous tries have had.

"Hey, you there yet?" Chris asks through the phone.

"Yeah. I'm in the parking lot, and the *warden* just greeted me. Listen, I'm late …"

"He greeted you in the parking lot? Okay, well, anyway, call me when you've completed the exam, okay? And you're *sure* you're okay?"

"Like the warden said before he barked into his cell and sped off, I'm 'a *professional* in the field of medicine.' Listen, gotta go. And hey, thanks. I'll be fine."

"Yeah, I know. You need to do this. Good luck."

Jon produces ID at the infirmary registration desk and overhears the guard on the other side of the glass make a call and ask why Doc Proffitt isn't there today. Hanging up the phone, the guard shakes his head and reluctantly issues Jon a temporary physician's badge. The desk guard then hands a slip of paper to an orderly, who eventually returns from the patients' record room with a thick file. Before the orderly releases the file to Jon, he's instructed to empty his pockets. Jon places his personal items in a plastic bowl which the orderly shoves inside an opening in a nearby bank of lockers. Jon's handed a white lab coat and a ticket to retrieve his belongings from the closed locker upon leaving. With the patient's medical file in hand, Jon goes in search of exam room three.

Jon notes multiple security cameras suspended from the ceiling throughout the infirmary. He realizes he should have asked Chris the exact protocol since he isn't able to find an alcove or desk where he can review the patient's file. He turns down a hall and spots a sign above a closed door. Room 3. He pauses in the hallway outside the room and opens the thick medical file. The dates and names he sees cause a lump to form in Jon's throat. He's glad he ran out of time this morning to grab breakfast.

It was just over a year ago, shortly after he'd gone into private practice, he'd stood outside an exam room and opened another patient's file. That file had only contained the patient's last name, which was Tart. Odd surname, he'd thought when he'd entered the room that day, concerned his staff hadn't collected more information on the patient.

Cornflower blue eyes flashed at him, and his heart flipped a little.

"Irish, what on earth are *you* doing here?" He spoke louder than he'd intended.

"*Doctor* Jon Elam." She sat on the edge of the exam chair and gazed at his name embroidered in red on a white lab coat.

He started toward her then paused, hoping she'd give the go-ahead for a hug.

She stood and walked to him. Placing her hands on his shoulders, she reached up and gave him a quick but sweet kiss on the cheek. She backed away with a low laugh. "So, I guess this is how all your patients greet you? Or just the women?"

"Just the ones named 'Ms. Tart.'"

"Sorry, I couldn't resist," Irish snickered. "And your staff has my actual patient file at the front desk for you. They were great when I told them this was more of a personal visit."

With a smile he motioned for Irish to sit while he used his foot to roll a low stool toward the exam chair. He remained standing, though, again waiting her approval before moving closer.

He regretted they weren't in his private office with the cushy chairs Sandy had picked out and the soft, indirect lighting. He wished he could show Irish how he displayed their families' pictures on his credenza. He thought about the picture of him holding Leesie at her christening and the one of Sandy and him with their arms around Leesie after she got Destiny for her birthday, and Gabe photo-bombing the tender moment as Irish captured it—actually one of the few pictures he had of Gabe.

But when he thought about it, given this was the first time they'd seen each other after so long and after the accident, probably better they were meeting in less memory-inducing surroundings.

"You sure are a sight for sore eyes, Irish. And before you say anything, I'm an eye doctor, and as part of my oath, I'm required to use that cliché at least once a day."

"Well, lucky me! And quite the eye doctor you are, *Dr. Elam.*" She patted the padded stool for him to sit. "So proud of you, you know. You established your practice so quickly after you and Sandy moved. But then you always were the smart one of the three of us, Gabe and I always said."

"Don't know about that." He eased onto the stool, but was unable to look at Irish when he asked, "How's Gabe?"

"He's struggling." Irish adjusted her skirt a bit nervously. "Speaking of Gabe, I don't have much time for this visit. He doesn't know I'm here, of course."

"I wondered." When he realized he'd unconsciously leaned in, he straightened his posture. Irish reached for his arm.

"It's okay, Jon." Her voice softened. "Right now, I need your emotional support as well as your medical advice and help."

The first time he'd laid eyes on Irish was in high school, and he'd physically ached. Her hair was long and blonde, and her eyes were big and an indescribable blue, and her chin was so narrow it made her face look almost heart shaped. She'd been standing at a hall water fountain looking about as lost as anything he'd ever seen.

He'd started to saunter across the hall toward her when he realized she wasn't at all lost. Her eyes were following Jon's best friend who was walking into the gym. Gabe's jacket was thrown over one shoulder, hooked on two fingers, the thumb of his other hand tucked into his back jeans pocket.

Jon's two-second shot at Irish Evans was over. Done. Finished. Kaput. In reality, he never had a shot at Irish. She already had *her* eyes on Gabe. Jon ribbed Gabe that things would have been totally different if Irish had first seen the better-looking of the two. To which Gabe said something like, "Oh yeah? Well, she did! She's not blind ya know!" They'd landed punches on each other's arms like teenage boys do goading one another. Jon still liked to think his weren't deliberate blows.

"I don't know how much Sandy may have shared with you," Irish began, bringing Jon back to the moment. "As a favor, I asked her to keep my coming here confidential." She half smiled. "But I'd understand if she told you in advance I was coming to see you."

"Sandy hasn't said a word, Irish."

Irish rubbed her bare forearms with her hands. "I'm sorry, Jon, could you make it a little warmer in here? Good thing your patients don't have to undress for their exams!"

He'd been so happy to see her, he only then noticed how thin she was. She'd obviously lost weight after the accident and trial, and after he and Sandy sold the house to Willa and Evan.

He jumped up and adjusted the thermostat. "Here, take my lab coat. Gee, you're shivering."

"I should have worn a sweater, but I'm mostly just anxious. You see the only way I know how to ask for your help is to just tell it like it is. That's what I did with Sandy and my parents, and my brother Michael. Of course, Gabe's been on the journey with me since I first became ill."

What the hell? Before he spoke, he willed his voice to remain calm and not show his growing concern. "Irish, anything I can do to help, you know all you ever have to do is ask."

Irish sat with his lab coat over her shoulders, holding the lapels in her hands which were crossed over her chest, and told her friend about the battery of tests, chemotherapy, the oncology visits, and soon hospice services. Did he know MJ? Yes, he said. He knew she was an amazing nurse, a pillar of the Fallow Ridge medical community and that no one knew more about end of life … . He thought he might be sick to his stomach.

"Jon, before I tell you how you can help me, I'm going to have to ask you to please hear me out. I can only imagine what your initial reaction will be. But can you please try and hold judgment?"

"Well, Irish, I don't know. I can certainly try. But after all, this is a lot to take in, as you can imagine, and without knowing what it's all about…" He took a deep breath and forced a smile. "Of course. For you, Irish Hart, anything."

"Thank you, Jon. I knew I could count on you. Cooder Ward is going blind."

Jon crossed his arms and listened while Irish explained in layman's terms the murderer's medical condition. Finally, she took Jon's hands in hers. "And here's where I need your help, Jon. I want to donate my eyes, my corneas, whatever is possible, to Cooder Ward."

Jon bit his lip to keep from saying something he'd regret. He looked at the ceiling to keep his eyes from giving away his immense sadness, anger, and fear.

"Jon, please, will you *oversee* the transplant?"

He couldn't help but look at her when she made the "oversee" pun. Her eyes seemed to ask her friend to acknowledge her feeble attempt to lighten the dismal situation they found themselves in. Jon managed to lift a corner of his mouth.

Jon squeezed her hands before he stood and paced the room. He promised to get back to her with more information and, yes, he assured her, he would personally take care of all the arrangements and perform as many of the procedures as he was qualified for. He had a colleague, a renowned ophthalmologist, Dr. Chris Proffitt, who also happened to be a friend of the prison warden. And, of course, he added, as he approached the examination chair to stand near her again, he would respect doctor-patient confidentiality.

"So, Gabe … how's Gabe with you, you know, donating your eyes to … I'm sorry, that's really none of my business, Irish."

"Oh, Jon, it's *every* bit your business." Irish looked into Jon's eyes then lowered hers. "The afternoon I shared my plans with Gabe, we argued. He stormed out and took off in the truck, with Destiny, and I didn't see them again until after dark. And yes, I almost changed my mind about the donation, almost told him that night I was wrong to even consider such a thing."

Irish used the chair arm to steady herself when she attempted to stand. Jon wasn't sure what to do—assist her? Or let her independence run free like always. He stayed within reach, in case.

"But, Jon, something in me believes if I can somehow help the man who killed Leesie, the person who will be helped the most is Gabe."

Jon thought for a moment, but had to confess, "Sorry, Irish, I don't understand."

"No, *I'm* sorry! Of course, you couldn't understand because it's all a bit crazy, I suppose. The day I shared the donation plan with Gabe, I also asked him to promise me he'll see Cooder Ward in prison after the eye donation. No surprise, I'm still waiting to hear Gabe make that promise. But when he does promise, which I honestly believe he will give me his word, then you know as well as I do, Gabriel Hart will not break his promise. And God willing, once he keeps it, he'll begin to move through his grief."

Jon stood speechless, trying to process Irish's reasoning. He watched her slip his lab coat off of her shoulders and hesitate before handing it to him. For a brief moment, he thought maybe she was wishing like he was that they were all back in the hall outside the high school gym. Back when innocence ruled. Back when their biggest problem was dreaming up something fun to do on Saturday night.

He followed Irish to the door where she turned to him. "Jon, it's just been so much for Gabe. If you can, and I don't know if anyone could, please don't take it personally, him ignoring your calls and avoiding you. You'll *always* be his best friend. He just has so much grief, and there you were, the first to get to Leesie and the last to see her alive. He'll come to his senses. I just know it. Once he sees Cooder Ward. And when he does, I hope you'll be there for him. I hope you can be there for each other."

Irish moved for the door, but Jon reached past her. "Irish, please, may I drive you home? Or at least walk you to your car?"

"No, but thank you, Jon. Mother's in the waiting room." Irish's hand landed lightly on his. "Just remember, one day Gabe will be ready to hear it … ."

Jon stood in the doorway watching her disappear down the hall and through the exit to the waiting room. The exam room door closed with a deafening thud.

## SIXTEEN

### COODER – Doc du Jour

The intense pin-sized light probes Cooder's right eye, his left eye, his right eye again. *Click.*

He whispers thank you to the darkness and loosens his grip on the arms of the examining chair. The doctor remains seated while he rolls the stool across the floor to the other side of the room. A louder click and stark fluorescent light from overhead floods the room. Through squinting eyelids Cooder studies the back of the doctor's head and wonders about the notes he's making on the thick medical file balanced on his lap.

The doctor killed the lights first thing when he entered the exam room so Cooder didn't see the name on his badge. And now he can't remember the name of the doctor the guard said would be examining him today. Dr. Proffitt generally examined Cooder, but there'd been one or two other doctors over the last year.

Cooder had noticed most doctors, even Dr. Proffitt, tended to be a little uppity, at least around him. Of course, they never made personal comments to Cooder, but they also never looked at him straight on, except to examine his eyes.

So far Cooder hasn't seen this doctor's face, but figures the "doc du jour," one of Bo's expressions, will be like all the others.

But Cooder'd decided, way back when he got the bad news about his diagnosis that he'd be grateful for any doctor who helped him, even if it was the last thing on Earth the doctor wanted to do—help a man who killed a little girl. Bo told Cooder that doctors take an oath to medically ease the pain of everyone—even murderers—but Cooder knew curing him had to set heavy on some doctors' hearts. It couldn't be easy to accept the fact a man like him could receive a corneal transplant when other innocent and way-more-deserving people would never regain their eyesight. Cooder struggles with the whole notion, too.

The doctor turns the stool slightly toward Cooder and places his pen in the chest pocket of his lab coat. He stares for a good while at the thick file on his lap. Cooder shifts in his chair. Maybe the doctor found a real problem. Cooder has been having a little fuzzy vision. And maybe the doctor doesn't know how to give him the bad news that something's gone horribly wrong since the last eye exam.

"The occasional slight blurring you experience," the doctor begins, lifting his head, "is fairly common following corneal cross- linking. Even after a year."

"Oh, *thank you*—"

"In *fact*," the doctor interrupts Cooder, "it appears the surgery on both eyes could not have gone better." The doctor pushes to his feet causing the stool to roll and collide with the wall, then releases Cooder's medical chart which falls heavily on the counter.

The doctor's face suddenly turns the color of a giant bruise, and Cooder draws a deep breath. They are the length of the room from each other, for which Cooder is grateful, but his eyes have cleared enough that he sees a huge vein bulge in the center of the doctor's forehead. The doctor's red-rimmed eyes are glaring at Cooder without blinking.

"So, with this examination I can authorize your medical release. That's what you've been waiting to hear, right? Well, want to know what *I* want hear?" The doctor glances at the large wall mirror then turns his back to it. "I need to hear you tell me what kind of a *man* ... No, wait, my ... my friend's right. You're not a man. You're a piece of ..."

The doctor shoves his hands into his pockets and paces, his eyes focused on the gray floor. He whispers, "I promised I'd walk in here and perform my professional duty. But you, *you murdered*—"

The doctor kicks the stool away from the wall, and it crashes loudly into the metal trashcan. The doctor turns again to the big two-way mirror and holds his hands in the air as in surrender.

"It's okay. I'm okay. We're okay."

Make no mistake, Cooder reminds himself, the doctor's words are not meant to reassure him. They're aimed at the guard monitoring the situation from the other side of the glass.

The intercom pops. "Doctor, you're *sure* everything's okay? I'm gonna have to call ... ."

"No. Don't call. I'm done here. Buzz me out. Now."

The doctor gathers the medical file and heads for the door. Cooder starts to breathe a sigh of relief when the doctor turns and marches toward him. Cooder's back pushes deeper into the examining chair as the tall figure approaches until the toes of Cooder's shoes, which were inches off the floor on the metal footrest, pit the crease in the doctor's pants.

"I promised I would see this through." The doctor speaks low. Cooder can hardly hear him. "Promised to do everything medically possible to ensure you regained your sight. But none of this, *none* of this, was ever about *you*. If I ever hear you say thank you again … *You* don't get to be *grateful*."

Stunned, Cooder watches the doctor exit the room. He covers his eyes with his hands. What the hell just happened?

A pull at his elbow causes Cooder to jump, fearful the doctor's come back to beat the living crap out of him. But it's the guard signaling with his thumb for Cooder to vacate the chair. "This ain't no Club Med."

"Hey, tell me," Cooder manages, dry mouthed, "that doctor who just left, what's his name again?"

"I dunno."

"Come on, help me out."

"Elam. Dr. Elam."

Cooder rubs the top of his head with sweaty palms. Cooder, you're an idiot. The friend he mentioned is Gabriel Hart. Irish talked a lot about Jon Elam and her husband being best friends since they were teenagers. Cooder should have recognized him from the trial.

After Irish visited Dr. Elam the first time, she'd told Cooder all about her plan and how she'd asked her friend if he'd do the corneal transplant surgery. As it turned out, Dr. Elam had consulted with Dr. Proffitt, who was a specialist in corneal transplants. Until today, Dr. Elam hadn't visited Cooder.

Cooder follows the guard out of the exam room. He looks down the hall and catches a glimpse of Dr. Elam turning the corner. Cooder's knees buckle as he thinks about Jon Elam on the stand the last day of the trial.

How Leesie's godfather broke down when he had to describe being the last person to see the little girl alive.

Cooder remembers it was late in the afternoon when Jon Elam was called to take the stand. All heads, however, turned to Leesie's dad who jumped from his seat in the gallery. Gabriel Hart pushed past his best friend, who was walking to take the stand, and stormed out of the courtroom, slamming closed behind him the big wooden doors.

Unable to look at Jon Elam while he gave his testimony, Cooder had kept his head lowered. Jon Elam's recounting of the moments following the accident, for Cooder, was the most painful part of the whole trial. After Cooder left the scene of the accident, he'd actually tried to sober himself up and picture what was happening at the end of the driveway. His imaginings included one where a little girl sits up, brushes herself off and climbs back on her bike; in another the only thing he'd hit was a bike, which had been left at the end of the drive. Neither scenario, however, was true.

The prosecutor had asked Jon Elam to share with the court Leesie's last words. The question was met with silence. The judge asked the witness if he needed a moment. Would he like a drink of water? Jon Elam was asked a second time to repeat Leesie's last words, but again the question went unanswered.

Cooder had gripped his thighs and closed his eyes and pictured Jon Elam holding Leesie's small head in his lap and prepared himself to hear how the little girl described the dirty blue car and the ugly man driving it.

Jon Elam had cleared his throat twice before uttering his goddaughter's final words. It was as if he'd channeled her, each word spoken the way they might have sounded whispered with a final breath. The words were barely audible yet deafening with childlike goodness and innocence. Cooder was overcome, as was apparently everyone. For an unbearably long span of time, within the confines of those solemn dark paneled walls, the only sound was that of folks sniffing back tears.

Once Cooder learned that the last thing Leesie Hart said wasn't about the awful man who ran her down, he understood why the prosecutor had pushed Jon Elam's testimony to the end of the trial—to get every ounce of sympathy from the courtroom.

And it did just that. The judge eventually quieted the room, but before that people in the gallery could be heard murmuring amongst themselves. How sad that Leesie's daddy wasn't in the courtroom. Why yes, that must have been why Gabriel Hart had stormed out the way he did. Poor thing, he couldn't bear to hear his little girl's dying words even one more time.

Cooder, too, assumed Gabriel Hart had to have already known what Leesie said. But within a few months after Irish began visiting him in prison, she'd confided that Gabe didn't have any idea what Leesie's final words were. Gabe had cut off all ties with Jon—angry that Leesie's godfather was the last person with her when it should have been him, her father. The best friends hadn't exchanged one word, not because Jon hadn't tried, since moments after the accident happened.

After the exam, Cooder returns to his cell and wonders if Dr. Elam ever got the chance to tell his friend what little Leesie said. After all, he'd called Gabriel Hart his friend that morning, so maybe. But no, the doctor had paused on the word friend, like a person does when they aren't sure whether they've got the right word, or if they do, whether they should they use it.

Cooder sits on the edge of the prison bed, his head buried in his hands. He remembers how Irish had been at a loss to try and find a way to get through to her husband. He shut her down every time she attempted to tell him what his friend shared at the trial.

She confided to Cooder that more than once she'd wanted to scream the words at her husband. But they were their daughter's precious final words, and they deserved better than being shouted in anger.

One day while she and Cooder Ward sat on opposite sides of the visitor glass, she said, "Gabe's like a judge who ruled testimony inadmissible because he holds a personal grudge against the witness. It's not fair. And that's not at all like Gabe."

She paused. "Cooder!" Irish had nearly dropped the phone receiver as she realized something. "Wait. It's not about *Jon*. It's not about Gabe shooting the messenger. It's about *what* our daughter said." She'd looked into Cooder's eyes. "Gabe's afraid *he's* guilty of Leesie's death."

Stretched out on his prison mattress, Cooder reckons he might never know how Gabe Hart could think *he* was guilty. He wasn't driving the car that struck down his little girl.

Cooder suddenly thinks about his momma and her reaction when he'd been arrested. She'd passed unexpectedly barely a month later. Her heart gave out, so he'd never know for sure, but it seemed, now that he thinks about it, the fact she went downhill so fast was because she was carrying around a lot of guilt about her son. He'd let his momma down after every binge and DUI. Even after he swore on the night of the shooting star when he was six years old that he'd never let her down again.

Maybe some parents think whatever their children do, regardless of how old their kids get to be, the mom or dad are ultimately responsible.

Cooder rolls onto his side, into a fetal position, ignoring Bo when he calls from the next cell, "So, what'd the doc du jour have to say? Are ya gonna live?"

# SEVENTEEN

## GABE – Up to the Task

"Quiet, boy." Gabe grabs Destiny by the collar and leads him into the utility garage. After easing the door closed behind them, he stands in the shadows near the small side window to spy on Willa and Evan exiting the back door of their house. Before Gabe walked to the garage, he'd forgotten to check if his in-laws' car was still in their drive. Fortunately, something as simple as locking the back door to the house required the couple's combined concentration. They hadn't noticed Gabe.

Watching his in-laws, Gabe observes that over time couples sometimes begin to look alike and act alike. Both of his in-laws had the same stance, leaning forward from their lower back and turning their heads with their shoulders. They were the only couple he'd ever been close to who'd been married for decades. He tried to calculate just how many years they'd been together, gauging by how old Irish would be if she were alive, but it was too painful an exercise—Irish and Gabe would never grow old together.

Willa and Evan walk side-by-side to the beige Mercury Sable to load themselves inside. The car is parked with the hood facing the window where Gabe stands, so he has a clear shot of Evan opening the driver door at precisely the same time and rate of speed that Willa opens the passenger door. Like geriatric synchronized swimmers, they turn and aim their backsides at the front seat and fall backwards into the car. The car chassis sinks a bit.

Their feet disappear inside the vehicle and the doors close in tandem. Willa doesn't trust automatic door locks, and Gabe suspects Evan manually locked his door, too, to avoid an argument. Still in perfect rhythm, they reach above their shoulders and pull their seatbelts wide in front of them and then down. Both look to check they are properly buckled in.

Destiny bumps his head against Gabe's leg for a pet. "Are all humans that predictable, Dest?" The dog's head tilts at the sound of the Mercury's engine starting.

◉ ◉ ◉

Gabe turns from the window and stares at the 15-passenger van. In the light of day, he sees how thickly it's covered with dust and cobwebs. He grabs the large rag he'd set aside to stuff into the exhaust pipe and wipes the door panel to reveal the company logo. Willa and Irish were probably right. He should have gone back to work at some point.

Through one of the back side windows, Gabe studies the basket complete with grass stains on its leather trim. A small tree branch wedged where two wicker seams meet reminds him again of Leesie's flight and the challenging landing.

Last night's tinkering under the hood of the 1990 Econoline meant this morning he has no reason to believe the van isn't up to today's task.

Still he starts it, just in case. It hums like its old self. Oddly the sound makes Gabe feel guilty, like he's teasing the van into believing they're going on a balloon chase. He turns off the engine, climbs out, and eases the driver door closed with a bit more care.

The walls and shelves of the shed are filled with empty fuel tanks, inflator fan blades, fuel lines, burners, and upright frames. Each looks like it's been relegated to a retirement home long before it outlived its usefulness. Each is a critical piece of equipment needed to fly a hot air balloon. Now they collectively only serve as abandoned reminders of the adventure and allure of aviation and the sheer joy experienced by first-time passengers, like Leesie, and obsessed pilots, like him. For a moment, he thinks he catches the scent of propane, ode de balloon pilot, Irish called it. But it was just lingering vapors from the van's exhaust.

He moves to the workbench in the back of the building, in search of a small tin, but quickly realizes he won't easily find it among the piles of junk that seems to have accumulated all on its own. Under his brown flight bag, he spots the red breath-mint box.

The contents rattle inside the metal container as he pries off the lid. Shiny as the day they were placed inside are the last of the remaining lapel balloon pins.

He removes one from the tin and holds it up to the window. Irish was the one who noticed each section of a shamrock resembles a heart. "Perfect combination of our names!" she'd cheered, showing him the shamrock-shaped logo she'd designed.

The souvenir, as it turned out, became a favorite of balloon pin collectors. That thrilled Irish. At balloon rallies they'd see folks wearing the shamrock pin on their shirts, jackets, or backpacks. Balloon enthusiasts, who would see the logo on Team Hart shirts or the van, or approach them when they were inflating the balloon, would go on and on about how they loved wearing the pin. They said it brought them good luck.

On the workbench, Gabe finds a small, clear plastic bag filled with screws and dumps the contents. Using pliers, he snips off the stickpin from the back of the shamrock pin and slips the clover shape inside the little plastic bag. He double-checks the seal, then tucks the bag into a front jeans pocket along with his knife.

Mentally ticking through the list of things he needs to accomplish in the next few hours, which now includes an unanticipated visit to the vet, he's startled when his shirt pocket vibrates. He pulls out his cellphone and hits the off button when he sees the caller is Jon.

"Hello?" The voice he hears is muffled.

Gabe stares at the phone screen. Did he hit the wrong button? He speaks into the phone, in an icy tone, "Yeah."

"Gabe?" The voice is still faint.

"Yes."

"Gabe, it's me."

His hand trembles as he pulls the phone from his ear and studies it. That voice. It wasn't Jon nor had it come from his phone. No, it couldn't be. "Irish?"

Standing at the other end of the building, Destiny whines and scratches at the side door. Gabe looks for the dog, willing himself yet again not to get hopeful that Irish has spoken to him. But again maybe Destiny is acting strange because Irish is there?

Destiny's howl reverberates off the walls and the balloon van at the sound of tapping on glass. Gabe spins around, hitting his shin on the inflator fan. In pain, he grabs his leg. *"Irish?"*

"Gabe? Here at the window. Son, it's Evan."

# EIGHTEEN

## EVAN – Windows to the Soul

"Evan, go on now and see what Gabe's up to," Willa insists just after Evan starts the car. "I don't like the looks of it. Not at all. He hasn't been in that garage in three years. Go peek in the window."

Before Evan can squeeze out from under the steering wheel, she adds, "And you know, Evan, no time like the present. Let's do this now." Willa pops open the trunk lid using the button inside the glove box. "It's better if just you give the package to him. Gabe was plenty put out with me this morning."

Halfway to the garage Evan glances back at Willa waiting in the car. She'd said "let's," which in his mind meant both of them before she conveniently remembered Gabe hadn't been pleased to see her earlier in the morning, so this errand is apparently now up to just Evan.

Walking to Gabe's driveway with parcel in hand, Evan tries to imagine his son-in-law's reaction when presented with the brown paper package.

For the life of him, Evan has no earthly idea how Gabe might react, and in his mind, Evan is to blame for that.

His first parish after theology school, decades ago, had been a small one, out in the country, 20 miles or more down Route 11, where they only met the first and third Sunday of the month. At the close of each service, parishioners sang a final hymn while he passed through the center aisle and out the front door to the top of the wooden church steps, where he shook their hands before they headed home for Sunday dinner. "Reverend Evans, won't you please join us? We're having fried chicken, mashed potatoes with gravy, green beans, and lemon meringue pie." The menu was always tempting, but he'd discovered that the person with lowered eyes who held their handshake a second longer than expected would later be waiting for him in the gravel parking lot.

Counseling those stoic souls who were brave enough to ask him for help, Evan realized then why he'd been called to the ministry.

That calling had remained his belief until his retirement a year ago. As he'd fully anticipated, once the congregation grew comfortable with the new minister who'd replaced him, Evan received fewer and fewer counseling calls, though he did still have a couple of regulars.

For the last few months, Evan's been wrestling with the notion that he never ever really eased anyone's suffering. But then when he thinks about it clearly, and remembers faces, and tears drying and smiles emerging, he knows he made a difference for some. He does, however, continue to ask during his prayers how he can help comfort a young man he loves like a son.

"Have faith" is the answer he receives, time and again.

Willa, however, doesn't seem to find solace in faith as often as he does. The good thing is Willa's plucky personality allows her to talk about their son-in-law openly to him.

They both agreed Gabe is pulling further and further away. Since their daughter died, Gabe has stopped calling his in-laws Mom and Dad. In Willa's own inimitable way, she once said that Gabe is making her feel "excommunicated."

Willa and Evan have also agreed if they mention their concerns to Gabe, in the emotional state he's in, he'll most likely see them as needy old people. Sure, they're old and needy—they need him in their lives.

Still their apprehensions go much deeper.

After Gabe and Irish were married, it took about a year for Gabe to begin calling his in-laws Mom and Dad. They all understood it was foreign to Gabe, who didn't actually remember having anyone in his life to call Mom and Dad.

Evan recalls how moments after Michael and Scot's beach wedding, he and Willa had clomped through the sand to congratulate Michael's husband, their new son, Scot. "Mom and Dad" floated off Scot's tongue like he'd been rehearsing his whole life for just that moment. Sadly, wishing the same for Gabe doesn't make it so.

Yes, their concerns now are much more than Gabe no longer calling them Mom and Dad. Now Gabe barely speaks to them. Willa and Evan are at a loss as how to reengage Gabe.

Package in hand, Evan maneuvers his way behind the evergreens overtaking the side of the utility garage. He feels silly and thinks he should have simply knocked on the side door. But he knows Willa is watching and will never let him hear the end of it if he doesn't follow her instructions about something this important. An errant branch snags the twine tied around the package he carries, but Evan manages to jerk the parcel free, like from a thief, and holds the package close to his chest.

My stars, Evan thinks, as he stands on his tiptoes peering through the filmy garage window. Evan sees Gabe busying himself doing something at the workbench with Leesie's car seat right at his elbow. Gabe's arm nudges the car seat, but he doesn't seem to even notice.

That small observation is a revelation to the retired minister. Evan knows the story from Irish, about the accident, how the car that young Gabe and his parents were traveling in skidded to a stop after being rear-ended and pushed sideways across the interstate, and how his father had miraculously removed the child's car seat with Gabe still strapped in and carried the toddler to safety on the wide grassy median. Gabe's father had run back for his unconscious wife, and while he unhooked her seatbelt, a semi's brakes locked in a desperate effort to stop. The truck jackknifed and crashed into the passenger side of the Harts' car. Gabe's parents were killed instantly.

We are a product of what we experience, Evan remembers, and how we process those experiences. He once read how infants, before they develop language, are informed through action. Evan can only imagine how the toddler internalized the actions his dad took the night of the accident, as the young man responded selflessly with life-and-death purpose, most certainly overcome with feelings of love and fear. Those traumatic moments had to have influenced Gabe's formative years.

But Evan also understands that just because he himself gains new clarity, that does not make Gabe any closer to accepting he was not responsible for anything that happened to Leesie or Irish. Or his parents.

Evan, of course, doesn't know the person or persons who were at fault for the deaths of Gabe's parents, but he does know who was guilty for Leesie's death, and that man is locked behind bars.

But Gabe, Evan recognizes, is locked in his own prison. His self-imposed punishment is to close himself off—to the best of his ability—to any loving relationship.

"Gabe, my son, when will you make peace with yourself," Evan whispers to himself before he calls to him through the window.

When the side garage door opens, Destiny bounds to greet Evan who is squeezing out from behind the shrubs. Gabe appears next looking like he hasn't slept in days, just the way Willa had described.

"Good morning, son," Evan greets Gabe.

"Evan, well, I didn't expect … you know, Willa was over earlier."

"Yes, yes, she was! Well, when she got back home she realized she'd forgotten to give you this." Evan extends the package to Gabe. "So, what are you doing with the van, son? Might not hurt to open the big garage door. Are those gas fumes I smell?"

Gabe neither answers Evan's question nor takes the package from him.

"Oh, I suppose I could have put the package on your back porch." Evan's chubby cheeks lift with a smile. "But you and I know Willa would never stand for that. So, if you don't mind, I'll just leave it with you." Evan again offers the soft package to Gabe.

Destiny, who had run to encourage Willa to get out of the car and join the family, has returned and is sniffing the bundle. With his front paws pressed against Evan's waist, the dog's wagging tail leaves no question that the package contains something familiar. Destiny nips at the string until Gabe grabs the dog's collar and leads him to sit.

"Evan, I know what this is, and I don't want it. Not now. Not ever."

Gabe's expression shifts from narrowed eyes to raised eyebrows. His son-in-law, Evan imagines, regrets his tone but not his words.

"Gabe, son." Evan takes half a step forward, adding in a lowered voice, as though sharing a secret, "Just because you take it doesn't mean you have to open it, ever."

Evan looks over his shoulder to see that Gabe's eyes are focused on Willa, who is fortunately still in the front passenger seat of the car, her hands cupped around her eyes like she's using imaginary binoculars to observe them. It wouldn't surprised Evan if Willa wasn't heading their way, having changed her mind about who should make the delivery.

"Willa thought it best," Evan says, again facing Gabe, "if she just waited in the car, and if I were the one to bring this to you, alone. She was afraid she'd upset you this morning when she brought breakfast over. Listen, Gabe …"

A breeze stirs a small clump of leaves gathered on the door stoop. Destiny pulls at his collar to try and catch a leaf between his teeth.

Evan is grateful for the distraction. He realizes he'd been close to sharing with Gabe the revelation he'd had while spying on his son-in-law through the garage window—that Gabe is in no way responsible for any of the four deaths that had so devastating an impact on his life. He is a victim of his parents' deaths, his daughter's death, and his wife's death. He was not the *cause* of any of them.

"Hey, boy, what do you have there?" Evan uses his free hand to remove a leaf stuck in the fur between Destiny's eyes and feels the package slip from his other hand. He is relieved to see Gabe shove the parcel under his arm.

Destiny, free from Gabe's grasp, jumps around until Gabe shoes him into the garage. Evan assumes his son-in-law is following the dog inside the garage until Gabe tosses the parcel on a stack of newspapers inside the door, steps back out, and closes the door behind him.

Evan wants to hug the dickens out of his son-in-law but thinks better of it, and instead extends his hand to Gabe. Men accept a handshake a lot more readily. Some men lean in and put their open hand on the other's shoulder, sometimes adding supportive pats. Those man-to-man displays of respect and affection are customary and don't seem out of line. If not for Evan's determination to find a way to reach Gabe, he might have given up and shoved his hand into his jacket pocket, so much time elapsed with it awkwardly hanging in the air between the two men.

But finally Gabe wipes his palm on his jeans and offers his hand to Evan. For Evan, the handshake is more than a perfunctory act. Regardless how Gabe feels or what he thinks, Evan is suddenly hopeful.

Evan, however, remembers his and Willa's fear of never appearing too needy, so he loosens his grip. To Evan's surprise, Gabe's thumb presses more firmly.

Later, when Evan climbs back in the car and Willa bombards him with questions, he doesn't share how it was good she'd insisted he peek through the garage window, how it helped him gain new insight into Gabe, and how he believed their son-in-law struggles with deep feelings of guilt and regret. The only thing Evan offers Willa are his empty hands as proof that Gabe has the package.

"The eyes are the windows to the soul," Evan thinks aloud.

"Evan, what on earth are you talking about? Are you quoting *Shakespeare?*"

"Oh, I don't know. So, Willa, where's our first stop?"

Evan was right not to share with Willa everything about his encounter with Gabe. She'd never understand how those last moments unfolded. But Evan does, and he is confident Gabe does, too, and that is all that mattered.

When Gabe prolonged his handshake with the touch of his thumb, Evan was taken aback, but he did the only thing he knew to do. He gazed unwaveringly into his son-in-law's increasingly red eyes.

Where they'd stood, dry leaves swirled around their feet, but not a word passed between the two men. Evan, however, saw Gabe's eyes tell him how sorry he was.

And when Gabe released his grip and lowered his eyes, Evan Evans urged silently, please, Gabe, look at me one more time, look into my eyes. Finally, Gabe had looked, and Evan's eyes were able to silently offer his love and reassurance. Son, there's nothing to forgive.

# NINETEEN

## IRISH – Pinstriped Broadcloth

Grandfather Lord was killed when my mother was three months old. I never asked Grandmother how she got the news, whether it was in the middle of the night with pounding on the door awakening her from a deep sleep or pacing the floor worried yet another night her husband wasn't home. But the *Piney Valley Messenger* ran accounts of the trial, so when my brother and I got old enough, we pored over old print articles at the library.

According to newspaper accounts, late on a Saturday night, Grandfather was riding in a horse-drawn buggy with two of his buddies when an argument ensued over who would climb down to open a farm gate. Alcohol was presumed to play a significant role in the quarrel and his buddies pushing Grandfather out of the buggy. Moments later, one gunshot and bullet in the back, and Grandfather was dead. The two men were arrested and charged with murder, but a jury found both men innocent. A motive was never established, and a gun was never located on or near Grandfather's body.

My mother said she couldn't remember her family ever discussing the way in which her father had been killed or ever saying much of anything about him. But when my mother was six or so, she saw Grandmother Lord kneeling over a large rectangular piece of white muslin spread on the floor. A basket filled with cutout pieces of fabric arranged by shape set next to Grandmother.

My mother said she was immediately taken with the squares of blue pinstriped broadcloth strategically placed at the center of six-pointed stars. "Willa," my grandmother had said to my mother, offering a swatch of the fabric for her young daughter to touch, "This was your father's favorite shirt."

When my young mother spotted a soft package tied with red ribbon under the Christmas tree that year, she hoped it was what she thought it was. She said she couldn't tear open the package fast enough. And sure enough, there it was, the quilt. From that night on, she'd slept beneath the quilt when it was cold or kept it folded at the foot of the bed in the summer. The quilt helped her feel connected to her father, that he'd really been a part of her life, if only for a short time.

The quilt's repurposed fabric began to disintegrate about the time Mother became a bride. She'd wrapped the quilt in tissue paper and stored it in the cedar chest that was a wedding present. I saw the quilt once when I was about 16. Mother had so looked forward to unwrapping it and showing it to her granddaughter one day.

A few months after Leesie died, Mother suggested I make a memory quilt like her mother had. I wrestled with the idea for about a week. Finally, one night after Gabe went upstairs, I asked my dad to haul Mother's portable Singer over to our house.

I didn't sleep that night, wondering if I should forget the whole thing. Finally, I got out of bed before dawn and began to gather Leesie's little clothes, and when I held her pajamas and christening gown against my cheek and felt the soft fabric, I knew I had to make the quilt. Even when Gabe grew furious with me that next morning, I told myself to have faith, though it seemed every thread of the quilt would break every fiber of my heart.

When it became clear I wouldn't be around long enough to convince Gabe to accept the quilt, I wrapped it in brown paper and passed it along to my mother. However, I *never* intended for the quilt to be presented to Gabe today of all days, especially with the vet and prison visits. But bless her heart, I believe my mother's timing was perfect. And asking my dad alone to deliver the package, perhaps her greatest ever stroke of genius.

## TWENTY

### GABE – The Plan

Gabe steps back into the garage and glances at his cellphone. He has less than half an hour to make the 10 o'clock vet appointment. In the same way he hadn't factored into the morning a trip to the vet, neither had he expected a visit from his father-in-law. He wonders how much Evan shared with Willa when he returned to the car. Willa, no doubt, asked the poor guy a hundred questions. Gabe reminds himself that in seven hours he wouldn't have to worry about Evan, or Willa, or anyone else for that matter.

After a yearlong wait, a few hours suddenly seemed like more than he could endure. He *could* end it all right then and there. The van was ready. The rag to stuff into the exhaust pipe was right there. Just get it over with.

He looks at Destiny sprawled on the garage floor eyeing the package perched atop the stack of newspapers. Gabe could leave Dest next door. He has a key to Willa and Evan's house.

He plays out in his mind a scene with Willa and Evan coming home in an hour or two to emergency responders, possibly seeing Gabe carried out of the garage in a black body bag, and them later unlocking their door to Destiny jumping with excitement to see them.

No, not fair to Irish's parents. Gabe needs to stick with the original plan for ending it all. He needs to wait until late afternoon, after his in-laws leave for their weekly dinner with Michael and Scot. It was the first Tuesday of the month, and they would stay after dishes were cleared and play Scrabble or Rummikub. Gabe knows dinner and a game are still on for this evening because he declined Michael's invitation to join them. Like he always did.

At exactly five o'clock Gabe will turn on the van engine, wait one or two minutes and call 911. The van runs good now, and its emissions would be super toxic in the closed garage. Gabe will be gone in 15 minutes, tops. He's figured into his calculations that emergency responders would have to fight rush hour traffic. He was confident they will arrive too late to resuscitate him. Gabe's body would be removed before Evan and Willa, on the other side of town, finish dessert and set up the game.

"Hey, Dest, what say we go for a ride?"

Gabe scans the van one last time before grabbing the soft package, locking the garage door, and placing the key in his front jeans pocket with his knife and the shamrock balloon pin.

Destiny trots at Gabe's heels until they reach the truck parked at the top of the driveway. The dog's front paws scratch against the side of the old green F150 as Gabe tosses the soft package into the truck bed.

Gabe looks up at the overhanging branches extending from the golden maples towering either side of the drive. They remind him of giant angel wings. God, he thought, stop already with the crazy supernatural ideas this morning.

Gabe yanks open the driver's door, the only working door on the truck. Destiny jumps past him and plops down behind the steering wheel.

"Hey, bud, how about I drive this time." After a nudge to his hindquarters, Destiny moves across the frayed upholstery and places a front paw on the armrest dangling by a single screw from the passenger door. The dog reminds Gabe of a little old man in a fur coat excited about taking a ride.

Gabe pumps the accelerator three times before turning the key in the ignition. The truck grinds to a rough start. While the engine warms, Gabe turns on the wipers and watches leaves scatter from where they'd collected overnight on the windshield. One persistent straggler wedged under the passenger side wiper catches Destiny's attention. The dog paws at the air as the leaf swishes back and forth until his paw catches the latch of the glove box and its door pops open. Destiny barks at something that's fallen from the box onto the floor.

The something is a pink stamped envelope Gabe was supposed to mail for Irish a year ago. Along with everything else today, now he has to swing by the post office. He slips the envelope into his jacket pocket.

Easing the truck down the hill to the bottom of the driveway, Gabe notes the gas gage is below an eighth of a tank. God, what *else*? If he hurries, he can swing by Wendel Sulley's. Regardless, he has to *make* the time or run out of gas.

Cedar Branch Road to Gabe's left is clear. So, to save time and gas, he doesn't brake at the end of the drive and makes a wide right turn onto Cedar Branch to head north.

A black SUV traveling south veers to its right to avoid Gabe's truck crossing the centerline. Gabe slams on his brakes, his right arm flying out instinctively to brace Destiny. Gabe swerves the wheel and steers the truck to the right shoulder of the road. The passenger side mirror just misses his mailbox before the truck skids to a stop, its front wheels landing off the pavement and the front bumper inches from the embankment.

The black SUV slides to a stop on the opposite side of the road. The driver lowers his window and yells, "What the hell! You coulda killed me!"

Gabe sits stunned, his heart pounding. Destiny leaps over Gabe's lap and barks, his breath leaving puffs of vapor on the truck driver window. Gabe stares blankly ahead.

A station wagon approaches the SUV from behind. Looking in the side mirror, Gabe sees the SUV driver flip him off before he speeds away.

Destiny straddles Gabe's shaking thighs and licks his cheek repeatedly until Gabe shoes him over to the passenger side. Gabe closes his eyes and pounds his forehead on the steering wheel. "Irish, damn it, it's just too much, just too much … ."

Gabe knows. Without even stepping out of the truck, he knows the back tires had landed where Leesie's body had fallen three years before. He could feel it. He knew the pavement intimately. It was, after all, the same blacktop his knees fell to when he first saw Leesie, the same pavement he'd crawled across to reach his daughter when his legs could no longer hold him, shards of the pavement's asphalt imbedded in the palms of his hands. The very pavement he'd lifted her limp, lifeless body from, where he'd knelt cradling her in his arms one last time, his face buried in her tangled curls still smelling of strawberry shampoo.

Irish, too, he remembered, had crumpled to her knees when she finally reached them. Together they'd cradled their baby.

At some point the sheriff's department and EMT vehicles arrived, and Irish had gathered strength enough to explain to them they needed more time with Leesie. Eventually, Irish stood behind Gabe, holding him against her unsteady legs, her trembling hands stroking his hair.

"Gabe, we've, we've got to let Leesie go now … Please, Gabe … before her school bus gets here … before the children see … "

He'd argued, couldn't she see Leesie was going to be fine? She was just a little shaken up, just a little stunned. "Leesie, wake up now … " he'd begged, using the back of his hand to gently rub her cheeks, to bring back their rosiness. "Your bus will be here any minute … Come on, honey, listen to Daddy … "

It took both Irish and Jon, who Gabe later learned had come back down the hill with Irish, to pry his arms from Leesie's body.

Inside the truck, Destiny yaps, and Gabe lifts his head and opens his eyes to see in the truck's rearview mirror a blue Volvo round the curve approaching him. The Volvo slows, and when it comes even with Gabe's window, the driver lifts two fingers off the steering wheel in recognition. A safe distance ahead, the car eases off the road and onto the shoulder in front of Gabe's truck.

Gabe throws the truck in reverse. All four tires back on pavement, he shifts into drive and speeds past the Volvo before its driver door opens. Destiny, looking out the back window, lets out a cry.

Gabe's focus never strays from the road, but he can feel Jon's eyes follow him until the truck was out of sight.

# TWENTY-ONE

## IRISH – The News

I'd walked from the basement steps to our front entryway where I found the wooden door open. Jon and Gabe stood on the porch facing one another. I watched my husband push his best friend with both hands causing Jon to stumbled backward, catching himself on the porch railing. I ran out the door as Gabe took the porch steps two at a time.

It was Jon, Leesie's godfather, who'd found Leesie that morning. It was Jon who had to deliver the horrible news, the worst news you could ever tell a parent. I could never imagine the unbearable grief he felt.

I would later learn that Jon had sprinted the whole way up the hill rehearsing what he was going to say. Sandy had tried to quickly coach her husband. She was the second person at Leesie's side, having followed Jon down to the road after he ran out of their house next door shrieking over his shoulder, "Something … terrible … happened!"

I heard Gabe call as he ran down the hill to the street, "Leesie! Leesie, where are you, honey?"

Jon held my hand as we ran together behind Gabe. "Irish, oh God, Leesie…"

But my senses had shut down. I didn't hear anything else Jon said. I just knew. In the blink of an eye I'd mentally recounted that Leesie hadn't been in the kitchen when I'd passed through. And there'd been no sound of her up in her room or on the back porch with Destiny. I knew. Maybe it was the way Jon gripped my hand like he never wanted to let go, or maybe it was mother's intuition. Or maybe it was the empty, hollow pull at my groin, like I had felt all the times I'd miscarried. Or maybe I didn't feel any of those things. Maybe time has played tricks with my memory.

None of that, of course, mattered. The outcome remained the same. My daughter lay dead at the end of our driveway.

# TWENTY-TWO

## COODER – Mockingbirds

Cooder removes a book from the handful of items stored on the lone wall shelf in his cell. *To Kill a Mockingbird*. It was Irish's favorite book, and she'd given it to him special. He'd started reading it a few months ago, just the way he'd promised Irish he would once he got his eyesight back. He likes it, a lot, but it's slow reading for him. It helps that he's seen the movie.

The picture of Charlene he uses to mark his place slips from the book, and he grabs it before it can hit the floor. He studies a young Charlene, her brown eyes wide, her smile, and the way she held her hand a distance from her face to block the sun and how she filled out that low-cut white top her momma didn't want her to wear. He likes how she sat on one hip in those denim cutoffs, her bare legs out to one side. God, he thinks, years later and she still did it for him.

He's wondered more times than he can count, if sitting on that rock up on Fallow Ridge, Charlene had known all the heartache the man taking the picture would cause her, would she still have married him, if she hadn't had to?

Well, he'll be seeing Charlene this Sunday. He needs to recall the exact words the eye doctor used today so he can tell her. He thinks it was something like "the surgery couldn't have gone better." Cooder hasn't yet decided if he'l tell her what else Dr. Elam had to say. He guesses it'll depend on how Sunday goes and if there's time.

During their visits they either have too much or too little time together. Sometimes they can't cram everything they wanted to say into 20 minutes. They talk over each other, then laugh and let the other go on. Other times those minutes drag like he and Charlene are sitting at a diner counter, starved, and their words are a food order stuck in the kitchen.

And sometimes they both fidget like they have someplace better they want to be. For Charlene, he can understand. She has a whole world of other choices out there. But surely not Cooder. He'll never understand why he doesn't hold onto every second with Charlene like he might never see her again. He's just an idiot.

Charlene, he knows, might have trouble getting off work this Sunday. But she said she'd try real hard. He sure hopes someone in the lawn and garden department trades a day off with her. Foley's has a good policy—long as all departments were covered, she can switch days. And her supervisor, well, she's been great working with Charlene's schedule. She'll do her best, Charlene said, and Cooder knew she would.

Charlene's always done her best for as long as Cooder's known her. When she was 16, the Cunninghams had come on hard times, so she'd dropped out of high school and went to work in the meat department at the local grocery. She'd once told Cooder she never could stand that job—slabs of icy raw meat hanging from hooks in the walk-in freezer, so close together there was no way to move around without bumping into one. The whole thing, he knew, must have been pretty gross for a teenage girl, but she stuck it out, mainly because the pay was good and when meat hit the expiration date, the storeowner would tell Charlene, "We need to get rid of that roast (or chicken or chops) before the inspectors go and surprise us with a visit. Take it on out with you when you leave tonight, ya hear?"

The owner and his wife also helped Charlene with the cost of schoolbooks once she was able to attend high school at night. For Charlene's graduation party, they made the biggest lunchmeat platter Cooder'd ever seen, with piles of white bread, big bowls of chips, potato salad, baked beans, and a tub of iced soft drinks. The big two-layer cake had writing that said "Congratulations, Charlene!"

Her parents felt beholden to the owner, and when the family started to get back on their feet, they only shopped at J. J.'s Market, even when the big chain store went in next to the interstate and it seemed the rest of town was about to desert the family-owned grocery on Main Street.

Charlene's picture still in his hand, he turns it over to see what she'd written on the back. "C1, YOURS 4EVER, C2." She'd used red ink and made the O in 'yours' into the shape of a heart. "I love that both of our names start with a C," she'd said soon after they started dating. "Since you're *older*, you'll be C1. The only one for me."

He smiles thinking about that summer afternoon they met. From his uncle's driveway he'd called to the redhead with the bouncy ponytail and her girlfriend walking down the sidewalk, "Hey, you girls, wanna go for a spin?" He was applying Armor-All to the upholstery of his uncle's yellow Chevy convertible. He'd stood on the back seat. "Got a new set of wheels."

The girls giggled but continued on down the street. That had been a good thing because he hadn't had a clue what to do if they'd hopped into the front seat. It wasn't an hour later he'd bumped into the same girls coming out of the drug store. He held the door open for them, wishing he'd stop grinning like a moron, but the redhead smiled back and slipped him an empty gum wrapper. He unfolded it to the sweet smell of watermelon and a phone number penciled inside the wrapper.

He watched the girls step off the curb, but when the redhead looked over her shoulder at him, she no longer flashed a smile. He didn't know if she all of a sudden changed her mind, and maybe he wasn't supposed to call her later after all. That night, he picked up the phone a dozen times to dial her number but never could make himself call her.

The next day, he was back at his uncle's, cleaning out the garage. Covered in cobwebs and dirt, he dragged a full garbage can out to the curb.

"Hi." Her voice was just as velvety as he'd imagined. "I want to apologize."

"Hey there!" Wiping his hands on the front of his T-shirt, he added, "Apologize? For what? That should be me." He pointed to the yellow convertible. "That's not my car. It's my uncle's. Sorry."

"I know. I saw your aunt and uncle drive it home the day they bought it." She tucked a stray strand of hair from her ponytail behind her ear. "Anyway, I've never given a boy my phone number. My girlfriend agreed to walk back home the way we'd come, so I could give it to you. Then there you were at the store." She'd lowered her eyes. "But after I gave you the gum wrapper, I thought maybe I shouldn't have. And then you didn't call. I'm sorry. Momma always said a girl shouldn't make the first move."

Cooder called her that night, and every night after that, and they dated for a year until the day he heard Charlene say through the phone they needed to talk. He was convinced she was breaking up with him. But when they met the next day, that's when she'd told him she was pregnant.

She was so worried. But he wasn't the least bit upset. In fact, he couldn't believe their good luck. Together they decided to take on the world. Funny, he thought, how old they both acted, as though they *could* take on the world at 18 and 20. His uncle had loaned them the convertible for their overnight honeymoon.

They'd moved in with Cooder's momma till they could get a place of their own, then two weeks later, he awoke in the middle of the night to find Charlene's side of the bed empty. Small drops of blood on the linoleum floor led him to the closed bathroom door.

"Oh, Cooder." There were tears in her voice from the other side of the door. "I'm so sorry."

He can't imagine how it feels to a woman, losing a baby like that, let alone having it happen twice more over the years. And he also can't imagine why in the world he ever told Irish during one of her visits about Charlene's three loses, but he had, and Irish said she'd miscarried twice before she had Leesie. Said she'd felt like she'd let her husband down every time. When Cooder nodded, Irish said, "Maybe someday when your wife visits, you could ask her how she feels now about all of the losses. Trust me, Cooder, she's never forgotten."

Irish had been right. He got up the courage to ask Charlene one day, and she shared that on every anniversary of a loss, she knew how old the little boy or girl would have been and what grade they'd be attending and imagined what sports they'd play or what musical instrument they'd have picked up. That day, there'd been the same tears in her voice, and her eyes, but there hadn't been the shame he'd remembered hearing when she actually lost each baby. Charlene had even thanked her husband for asking her how she felt about never having children and placed her hand on the glass separating them. He'd placed his hand aligned with hers.

He reminds himself that when Charlene suffered the loss of a child, it was never her fault. She'd been a model mother-to-be, always getting plenty of rest, taking her vitamins, and never drinking alcohol. Cooder, however, was solely responsible for the loss of one little girl, Leesie Anne Hart.

On any given day and at any given moment Cooder Ward knows exactly how old Leesie would have been. What grade she'd have been in. That she loved her Barbie, her Destiny, and *The Wizard of OZ*. That she'd taken her first hot air balloon ride just before her ninth birthday. That's when she decided she wanted to be an astronaut when she grew up. That on her birthday, three years ago to the day, she'd gotten a shiny new bike. And that for Halloween that year she would have dressed as a unicorn.

There was only one day Cooder had been unable to instantly recall all the details about Leesie Anne. It was on what would have been her 10th birthday. That's when he awoke in a hospital room with barred windows and a guard at the door. He'd tried to move his arms, but they were strapped around him, like he was giving himself a bear hug. Prison guards had put him on suicide watch so he wouldn't try again.

Everyone assumed Bo had gotten the pills for Cooder, and he had. Bo just hadn't known it. Cooder had told Bo he couldn't sleep most nights, and each time he'd asked Bo if he'd finagle a couple of sleeping pills. Cooder had done that for months, saving up the pills, and then he took them all at once.

At first, only Charlene had been allowed to visit him in the infirmary. Then one day attendants removed the straightjacket, and Irish walked through the door. At that time, she hadn't been visiting him too many months at the prison, but there she was to see how he was doing. It was the first time since the trial he and Irish had been in a room not separated by glass. Irish handed him a package and apologized that it was mostly unwrapped. He could see it was a book. "Guards searched inside," she'd said with a grin. "They removed the file I stashed inside for your escape." He remembered he'd managed a smile.

Irish shared that day that she'd had the book for years and had read it five times. They'd made it into a movie, she'd said. Had he seen it? Well, she hoped he'd see it sometime *after* he read the book. Then she'd asked him to open the front cover and read aloud what was written there. "To Irish, All the best, Mary Badham 'Scout' 3/5/10."

Irish explained to Cooder that when the woman who'd signed the book was a little girl, she'd had played Scout in the movie. To Irish, the character Scout represented hope, and it meant a lot to her to have met the actress. Irish didn't want to ruin the story for Cooder, but she thought some of the characters in the book might also speak to him. He remembered thinking he knew a movie could speak to a person, but never knew a book could.

As it turned out, months later he went to the movie when it played at the prison. He told Irish about it afterwards, saying he hoped she wasn't mad he'd gone to the movie before he read the book. He hadn't been able to see too much on the screen because of his eyesight, but when he'd heard young Scout's voice, it made him think of little Leesie.

Irish had immediately asked Cooder what he thought about the man who was found guilty. Cooder said he was surprised. "After all, Tom was innocent. Sure, there were idiots who didn't like him because he was Black, but there was a good chance Gregory Peck would've gotten him off. And Tom *had* to know what'd happen if he was to run."

Cooder wasn't Black or innocent like Tom in the movie, but he kind of understood how Tom felt—he'd lost hope, and if he couldn't go back and change the events that got him where he was, he'd sooner die.

"I killed a mockingbird," Cooder remembers telling Irish that day.

"You're right, Cooder," Irish said on her side of the phone conversation in the visitor area, her eyes lowered. "There's no denying you did. But to my way of thinking, we're *all* mockingbirds—even you, way deep inside."

Since that day, he's thought a lot about what Irish said. She'd meant him trying to take his own life had been wrong, like killing a mockingbird.

Today, on what would have been Leesie Anne Hart's 12th birthday, he holds onto that thought long after he tucks Charlene's picture back into Irish's favorite book.

## TWENTY-THREE

### GABE – Obsessed

Gabe pulls into Wendel Sulley's on fumes.

Rolling until the truck's gas tank lines up with the fuel pump, he hears himself say, "Thank you." He can't remember ever having said thank you aloud with no one around. But he is grateful for having made it to the station.

He pumps five gallons, enough for the day, pays cash inside, and drops his change into a glass jar for Isabella, a little girl with leukemia. She obviously loves having her picture taken—she has an open giggle kind of smile with her hands stacked on top of her perfectly round baldhead.

Gabe parks on the street in front of the vet's office. Inside the truck, he holds Destiny's muzzle and kisses the dog's cold, wet nose. The dog's eyes dart back and forth between the building and Gabe. Gabe has made his decision. He will leave Destiny with Dr. Mac.

He's been sure this is the right thing to do, but now all of a sudden the pounding in Gabe's head has him second-guessing his decision.

Actually, when he thinks about it, hasn't his head been killing him since he almost caused an accident at the end of his driveway? Or was it when he saw Jon? For God's sake, why the hell did Jon have to drive by the house—today?

◎ ◎ ◎

*Gabe opened the front door, and Jon blurted out, "She's dead."*

*"Sandy?" Gabe asked, moving toward Jon to steady him and comfort his best friend.*

*The two friends had stood there as though suspended in time, while a brisk north wind whipped around the corner of the house and continued down the full length of the front porch, and the red swing swayed ever so slightly, until Jon cried, "No, oh, Gabe, no, it's Leesie. Leesie is dead."*

◎ ◎ ◎

Gabe pushes back tears from the unbearable memory and his lingering goodbye hug to Destiny in the few moments they still have alone. He is half relieved his phone rings to break the heart-wrenching moment. Then he sees the caller is again Jon. *Man, why can't you leave me alone today?*

Gabe's head is now in full pounding mode with all of the unanswered questions triggered by Jon driving by the house and now calling him. *So, Jon, why didn't you, with all of your medical training, stay with Leesie and send Sandy to fetch me? How could you have been so sure Leesie was dead? Did you try everything before you ran up the hill?*

Destiny licks a tear streaming down Gabe's cheek.

Halfway up the flagstone walk to the vet's office with Destiny in tow, Gabe sees the notice.

Gabe takes out his phone and dials the number printed on the sign. An overly cheery voice greeted him. "Good morning! The Pet Vet's office! Where Dr. Mac is every animal's best friend!"

"Right, hi, this is Gabe Hart. Sorry, didn't know you guys moved."

"No, *we're* sorry for the inconvenience! Are you at our old office? Do you see our new address on the sign?"

"Yeah. I'll get there as soon as I can. Hey, can you tell me who made the appointment for today? Or what number you called to confirm?"

"Happy to, Mr. Hart! Please hold while I look that up."

"Hey, you know what, it doesn't matter. I'll be there soon."

"Great! Hey, Mr. Hart, while I have you, could I ask a question?"

"Sure."

"Do you still give hot air balloon rides?"

"No. And not likely to."

"Oh, okay, I see. I just wanted to give my boyfriend a ride for his birthday. But I understand. See you in a bit!"

Gabe slides the phone into his jacket pocket, piles Destiny back into the truck, and heads to the new vet office on Cobbler Street. He knows the town like the back of his hand, but accidently turns one street too soon onto Walnut Street, the last street he wants to see.

# TWENTY-FOUR

### Mrs. Hisey – Walnut Street

As it happened, I'd only just transitioned this morning from human form when dear Irish set out on her day trip back to Earth. Wish I'd had the opportunity to send with her the best of luck today. Goodness. What a time Gabriel's had.

They were such a dear young couple, Irish and Gabriel. He was a strapping young man and reminded me of my late husband back when we first met during World War II. Gabriel seemed to appear out of nowhere whenever I needed something moved or repaired. Oh, and Irish was such a sweet girl. She brought me fresh flowers every Saturday after she closed up Smiths' florist shop. The couple were newlyweds when they rented the apartment above the drug store that my husband and I owned.

My husband was a pharmacist, and I was a registered nurse, so the drug store did quite the business when we opened and word spread that if you didn't understand what your doctor prescribed or diagnosed, between Mr. Hisey and me, we could answer a lot of questions. The flu outbreak of

'56 hit the area hard, and there were countless sick children. I'd learned a few remedies during the war that helped relieve stomach symptoms. Parents wanted their babies to feel better, and there was nothing I wanted more than that for them, too.

It was Mr. Hisey's idea to call the store after the location instead of our surname. Hisey Drugs, he thought, sounded odd, like maybe the name was High Sea Drugs. Folks might think if they came in the store they were heading into rough waters, he'd laughed. So Walnut Street Drugs it was.

I had misgivings about the location at first because the store was only a block from the jail, and we lived over the drug store. I wasn't as worried during business hours. Guess I assumed if a prisoner escaped it would be at night and they'd come murder us in our sleep. But we installed security cameras, such as they were back then, given the narcotics my husband kept in stock under lock and key.

After my husband died, a nice young pharmacist, Terry Butt, fresh out of school, leased the store. He and his wife had just bought their first home on the edge of town, so they had no use for the upstairs living area. I converted two former downstairs storage rooms into my own apartment and added a full bathroom with a shower *and* a tub onto the back of the building. I had tenants upstairs twice before the Harts moved in.

And then there was Leesie. Oh, my. Do I ever remember the morning she came into the world.

◉ ◉ ◉

"Irish!" I'd heard Gabriel call. He'd left their upstairs apartment door open. "It's two in the morning, and anyway you don't have time to put on mascara!"

"I'm not putting on mascara! It's eyeliner, and I'm not leaving the bathroom without it! Oh, oh! Oh, God … "

"Your suitcase is in the car, and if you don't come out, I'm coming in."

"No! You can't! Oh, Gabe, my water broke. I'm sort of scared."

I could hear their footsteps above me as they entered the upstairs hallway. I opened my door, debating whether to ask if they needed anything. "Breathe, Irish. Short breaths. Whew. Whew," Gabriel coached Irish.

"Gabe, so maybe I was foolish (whew whew) to put on eyeliner (whew whew), okay, and a little mascara."

"Lipstick choice was good though. Matches your robe." Bless his heart, Gabriel was trying to lighten the moment, but Irish wailed. I could hear her contractions were coming closer together. Too close together for them to make it to the hospital.

"Gabriel, is it time?" I called upstairs.

"Yes, Mrs. Hisey." Gabriel paused while Irish howled. "Irish may not make it to the … "

"I'll slip on my housecoat." I added, "Irish, just breathe, dear, along with Gabriel. And, Gabriel, don't let her push until I get up there."

They were a sight when I got to the top of the stairs. Irish, big smudges under her eyes from the mascara and her back pressed against the doorframe to their apartment. Gabriel kneeling with Irish's purse slung over his shoulder. "Gabriel, why don't you go inside and call an ambulance and bring back with you some clean bed linens and towels. And, Gabriel, let's don't be too long."

Gabriel jumped to his feet and searched his front jeans pocket for the door key until he saw the door was still open. His voiced cracked but he managed a smile. "I'll only be a minute, Irish."

After he made the call, he helped me lower Irish's back to the floor and arrange a pillow under her head and towels beneath her hips. We draped a white double sheet over her bent knees. I held out my arm for Gabriel to help me to my feet.

"Where are you going? No, now wait, Mrs. Hisey … " Gabriel turned as white as the sheet covering Irish.

"Oh, I'm not going anywhere, Gabriel. I'll be right here with you. Now kneel down, yes, like that, and when you see the crown of the baby's head … "

Gabriel stayed focused in spite of his wife's moaning and only minutes later announced, with a mixture of panic and pride in his voice, "Irish, it's … it's a girl … "

"Is she okay? Why isn't she crying?" Irish asked. During her first trimester, she'd confided she'd had a little spotting, but unlike her other two pregnancies, the baby kept growing, and then one day Irish announced she'd felt a little fluttering. Eventually she felt kicking and was beside herself with joy. So, in that upstairs hall, Irish held her breath until a second later the baby's first gasp of life left no mistake she'd arrived with a healthy set of lungs. Gabriel swaddled their daughter and placed her in Irish's waiting arms.

Outside the ambulance arrived with sirens blaring. While the new family huddled on the second-story landing, I headed downstairs to greet the EMTs.

"Leesie?"

I paused surprised to hear Irish call me by my first name. I hadn't been sure she even knew it. I was always Mrs. Hisey to both Gabriel and Irish. I was about to ask if she needed something when Irish continued, "Oh,

Gabe, what do you think? Let's name our little angel after Mrs. Hisey. Leesie Anne?"

"It's perfect. Welcome to the world, little Leesie Anne Hart."

◉ ◉ ◉

Exactly nine years later I waited with Gabriel and Irish beneath the large oak tree in front of the jail. I'd gotten the terrible news, as had all of Fallow Ridge, and I hobbled on my cane down the street to the jail. I'm not sure Gabriel and Irish even knew I was there, standing within arm's reach. I'm not sure they were even aware other townsfolk had gathered to offer their support. Yes, of course, some were there out of morbid curiosity.

Irish held onto Gabriel's jacket. It wasn't clear whether she was supporting him or steadying herself. They stood in the light drizzle and stared at the side entrance to the jail.

The heavy door finally opened from the inside with a swoosh, and I heard Irish gasp and saw Gabriel charge forward. Gabriel screamed, "You son-of-a ... !"

My husband once shared a war story with me. A soldier had an emotional breakdown and sprang from a foxhole to avenge the death of his buddy who'd been killed not two inches from him. Sadly, enemy troops immediately captured the soldier. "Revenge lacks peripheral vision," my husband added somberly to the story.

And so it was with Gabriel. To detain him, officers forcibly seized his arms and pinned them behind his back. He was lifted up and hurled spread-eagle across the wet hood of a patrol car.

We all stood helpless, not knowing what to do. Gabriel's face was pressed against the car hood while brown uniforms swarmed around him and voices screeched over hand-held radios. From where I stood, I could see Gabriel's eyes follow the man in the orange jumpsuit.

Officers maneuvered the prisoner toward a squad car parked near the one where Gabriel was being restrained. A man in the crowd screamed "child killer" at the prisoner, and like a mob, others began yelling names and obscenities.

I'd nearly joined in the rant when it hit me the man in the orange jumpsuit had not yet had a fair trial, and I had already convicted him of murder. How had I felt every time I was prejudged—because of the color of my skin, and called a name and threatened with racial slurs when people had preconceived notions about me? I stood silent. Had I joined in the chanting, I'd have been just like those who had slung hateful words and made unfair assumptions about me over the years.

Before the prisoner was shoved into the backseat of the patrol car, those of us watching could see Gabriel was no longer struggling with the officers holding him down. His body wasn't limp as though he'd given up. Instead, his demeanor was that of a man confidently waiting it out on the verge of vengeance.

The sound of sirens could be heard trailing off in the distance and police radios squawking confirmation that the criminal had been escorted successfully outside the city limits. The officers released Gabriel.

The young couple, who nine years before had huddled together only a block away in an upstairs hall above a drug store, vowing to love and protect their little angel girl forever, now stood on a wet, cold sidewalk, facing one another as though they had no idea what to do next with their feet, their hearts, and their lives.

## TWENTY-FIVE

### COODER – A Gut Memory

From his cell bed mid-morning, still processing what happened during his eye exam, Cooder hears the faint sound of a prison wagon's siren. A new crop of prisoners, he thinks.

He recalls awakening to sirens his last day as a free man. He'd thought they were on a TV cop show. He'd pried his eyes open, curious as to why the sofa upholstery felt scratchy, when he saw blue lights flashing through steamed-up car windows. It was then the events of the previous day came rushing back to him in spite of his drunken stupor.

He'd borrowed his friend Farley's car, gone on a binge after six months sobriety, and at some point parked the car in an abandoned barn with half a roof.

But then he'd had a gut memory of a thud and a crumpled bike and buying what he'd hoped would be enough booze to hold him for a couple of days.

The booze he'd bought after the accident, he guessed, was to keep him in a stupor of denial. Because, yes, Cooder had been inebriated the morning he killed Leesie, but clearheaded enough to know what he'd done, and that he was wrong to stomp on the accelerator after hearing the thump and seeing in the rearview mirror a white angel balloon with pink and purple streamers float upward until it was caught in the branch of a golden sugar maple.

He could have, should have stopped, especially when he saw reflected in the broken glass of the passenger side mirror the bent frame of a pink bike, on its side, the front wheel still spinning.

"What kind of man," he once asked himself during one of Irish's visits, "doesn't stop when he hits a little girl's bike?"

He'd been so ashamed he'd asked the question aloud. He'd been totally out of line. He guiltily looked at Irish, not for an answer, of course, but to see her reaction. She was chewing on her right thumbnail, staring at the little ledge in front of her. In time, she spoke softly into the phone. "A man who rationalized that a little girl forgot and left her bike on the side of the road."

## TWENTY-SIX

### IRISH – True Regret

I think Cooder and I were equally surprised to hear his question and my answer. He'd sat back in his chair after he asked what kind of a man hits a child's bike and doesn't stop, like he was stunned to hear the words come out of his mouth. When I answered, to be honest, I didn't even know I had that thought. Together Cooder and I heard it for the first time.

Once I'd considered it, however, it seemed like a plausible explanation. Why hadn't the public defender ever acknowledged that as a possible scenario to reduce Cooder's charges?

I watched Cooder's reaction to my answer, and it seemed to me maybe I'd hit on the truth. Cooder's facial expression reminded me Robert Duvall's Boo Radley at the end of *To Kill a Mockingbird,* when Scout spots him cowering behind the open bedroom door where Jem lay injured.

"Cooder, is that what happened?"

He didn't answer. He'd simply hung up the phone and motioned to a guard that he was ready to leave.

Unable to sleep that night while replaying the scenario in my mind, I remembered the letter Cooder wrote us a few months after the accident. I got up and searched through the box of sympathy cards and handwritten notes until I found the unopened envelope addressed to Mr. and Mrs. Heart, with his name on the return address. I slid my finger under the seal and unfolded the single sheet of lined notebook paper. There were numerous eraser smudges and one small hole from too much applied pressure. The penmanship reminded me of Leesie's second-grade attempts.

The letter was short, less than half a page, and that included his small, scrawled signature. The misspelled words made me think he alone had composed the letter.

> Mr and Mrs Heart,
> You deserve your little girl. She deserves you.
> I did a terable thing. And Im sorry.
> I wish I could take yore daughters place.
> But you still don't have your little girl. Cooder Ward

To my knowledge, Cooder Ward had never asked for nor sought forgiveness. Not in his letter, not during our visits. I could only assume that was why he'd so abruptly ended our conversation earlier that day. All the rationalizing in the world concerning Cooder Ward's actions the day of the accident didn't change the fact Gabe and I didn't have our little girl.

True regret seeks no mercy.

# TWENTY-SEVEN

## GABE – The Vet Visit

"**G**abriel Hart! Good to see you, son. Right on time! Ten o'clock. But, wait who's *this*? Oh, I'm just kidding, Destiny! Who could ever forget *you*? How ya been, boy?"

Gabe always thought the veterinarian favored a clean-shaven St. Nick while Irish contended that in another life he was St. Francis of Assisi. Gabe thinks the man is a saint however you look at it, and whatever that might mean.

"Well, Gabriel." Dr. Mac rests his hand on Gabe's shoulder. "I never had the chance to tell you personally how sorry I was to hear about Irish. I'd ask how you've been this past year, but isn't that the dumbest question? People seem to feel obliged to ask it though."

Gabe half smiles. He estimates it's 100 degrees in the examining room, so he takes off his fleece jacket and hangs it on one of the straight-backed chairs.

"And Destiny," Dr. Mac chuckles, "how are you faring? Healthy as a *horse?*"

He's still snickering at his joke when a vet tech joins Dr. Mac to review Destiny's chart displayed on the computer screen.

"Hey, Dr. Mac, mind if I step out … uh, to make a call?"

"Sure, that's fine, son. Dest and I got this."

Gabe walks over to Destiny and takes his muzzle into one hand and pets his head with the other. "Hey, I'll see ya, boy," Gabe whispers, his voice cracking.

Dr. Mac turns. "Gabe, is everything alright?"

"Yeah, sure. Just need to make a call."

The receptionist, busy on the phone with her back to Gabe, doesn't notice when he slips out the front door.

Gabe sits in the truck with his hand on the key in the ignition. He's done it. Destiny will be in good hands. The best. Gabe saw to it. Or rather, Irish did.

Gabe can't seem to gather the energy to turn the ignition key or wipe his eyes.

"Excuse me, Mr. Hart!" The receptionist taps on the driver window, holding Gabe's jacket in her hand. "Your phone was ringing, so Dr. Mac asked me to bring it to you."

# TWENTY-EIGHT

## MICHAEL – We Have a Problem

"I swear, Michael, I'm going to take away your cellphone!" Livy has that high pitch thing going on in her voice. "Okay, I can't do that right *now*, but I promise, if you call again, I won't answer. I've *got* this. Good-*bye!*"

Michael can't help himself. He's called Livy three times while driving to his parents' house. Of all the days. He and Liv have a one o'clock meeting with Sage Foundation's new CEO. God, he thinks, a multiyear award from Sage would make *all* the difference; Home4Good could finally expand to outlying counties—who knows, the nation!

The foundation's CEO aged out of foster care at 18 and became homeless, so Livy won't have to convince *her* there are hundreds of undocumented "housing insecure" youth throughout the state. Or make a case that students are unable to get into homeless shelters because of bed shortages, so they sleep behind churches or in the woods, in tents, but *still* get up and got to school every day. Or that those same students linger after first bell to wash up when the school restrooms emptied.

He and Liv hear it all the time from suits. "Well, *we* don't have homeless students in *our* district." Oh, yes, they do. Even the smallest and most wealthy districts have dozens of homeless students. Fortunately, H4G's coaching and advocacy programs are working. It isn't that complicated—simply do for students in need what anyone would do for their own kids.

Michael smiles thinking about the text he and Liv got the night before from D. L., one of the first students their nonprofit served, now in college. He was just checking in to say hey and see if they could use his help that weekend with the new class starting. Later, when Michael and Livy saw each other in the office, they'd grabbed hands and done their traditional happy dance—they'd heard from one of their kids!

Michael turns into his parents' drive off Cedar Branch and stops at the bottom of the hill. He texts Liv, "Thanks." He and Livy, his colleague and best friend for ten years, were like two sides of the same coin. Michael knows she'll answer her cell regardless of the number of times he calls. They were always there for each other. He sees Livy reply. A smiley face. A second text follows: "pls call when u know something about Gabe."

Michael eases the car to the top of the driveway where Willa is pacing, wringing her hands. Her tartan plaid sweater falls from her shoulders to the pavement when she begins flapping her arms to signal her presence. Did she really think he can't see her if she doesn't flag him down? Michael has his work cut out for him. His mother appears just as stressed as when she called him an hour ago.

"Lord, Michael," she cried into the phone, "your father and I were driving through the cemetery gate when it hit me. I'd forgotten the calendar and the vet appointment! So, I told your father I needed to go home to take my arthritis medicine. Michael, how on earth could I forget the calendar? You know Irish and I planned—"

"Mom." Michael held the phone away from his ear, exasperated, trying to get a word in. "It'll be okay."

"Michael, I've messed up everything. And I can't tell your *father* about the *plan!*"

The plan. After Michael learned about the plan a year ago, he'd considered for half a second telling his dad. If Evan had known what his wife and daughter were cooking up, he'd have said the idea was over the top. Evan's view on the subject, of course, wouldn't have stopped Willa and Irish from going forward. But his dad didn't contain an ounce of deception in his body, and it's possible Evan would have alerted Gabe about the plot to ensure he went to the prison on October 1st. So, Michael never told his dad. How could he? Not when Irish had been so desperate to help her husband.

She'd called him one day to say Gabe was out, could Michael please drop by after work. The Castleton's first floor was empty, so Michael climbed the stairs to find his niece's bedroom door open. Through the doorway he saw his sister in a pink nightgown sitting on the edge of Leesie's bed, her thin hand running along the coverlet. She motioned for her brother to join her. He sat gingerly next to her on the bed.

"Michael, I need you to do something for me."

"Anything, Irish, you know that."

"I want Gabe to promise me something."

"And you want me to ask him?"

"No, Gabe and I've discussed the promise several times. Actually, I guess I've always done all the talking." She paused, the pictures lining Leesie's mirror catching her attention. She closed her eyes. "He hasn't promised yet, but I believe he will. What I need is for you to help him keep the promise."

"You know, Gabe's a man of his word, Irish, so I'm thinking if he makes a promise, he'll keep it. Right?"

"Oh, silly brother." She opened her eyes and rolled them at him similar to the way she had when he was 13 and she told him he was lousy at keeping it secret that he was gay. "I've asked Gabe to promise he'll visit Cooder Ward on Leesie's 12th birthday."

Michael's back straightened. He reached for her hand. It felt light and limp. "Irish, I know you've made numerous prison visits. And I think it's wonderful those visits helped you process your grief. But, Irish, I'm going to be honest with you. I'm not sure it's a good idea for Gabe to visit Cooder Ward ever, even once."

"I'm not sure we have a choice, Michael." He helped her stand and walked with her down the hall to her bedroom. She explained that Gabe was shutting down—sleeping in his clothes, forgetting to stop at the grocery, or to let Destiny out or in. What would happen to him when she was gone? Without Gabe having to face her every day, she feared he would no longer be able to face life.

Irish stopped beside her bed to rearrange the vase of fresh sunflowers she kept on the nightstand, then lowered herself onto the mattress. She let Michael lift her legs and pull the covers up to her shoulders. "Michael, if a promise can keep Gabe alive for a year, maybe when he faces Cooder Ward, he will face the truth."

Michael listened as his sister described her plan: the vet visit, the calendar reminder written in Irish's hand, the October 1 reveal with Willa feigning surprise at seeing an appointment for 10 o'clock.

Michael asked what his role was in the ruse. On cue, Willa bustled through the bedroom doorway, and Irish winked at her brother. He bent down, kissed his sister's forehead, and whispered, "Ah, yes, keep Mom on task. I'm on it."

But he didn't want to be on it. After the visit with Irish, Michael had expected Scot to agree with him that the whole plan was ridiculous. Scot, however, sided with Irish. He thought it made sense, that it might take something like an appointment to get Gabe out of the house to keep such a difficult promise.

Really? Michael scoffed. Didn't Scot know it wasn't the theory behind the plan that he opposed? It was the plot. It was lame. A vet visit was not going to send Gabe running out the door after three years to meet the man responsible for his little girl's death.

Scot hugged Michael. "I think you have to trust your sister on this. I know how much you love her and how you've always looked out for her, for your whole family, for all of us. That's who you are. You take care of people. But Irish is dying, Michael, and I have to believe there's something she knows none of us can understand right now. Not even you. And it's okay if you can't control or fix this."

And so that's how Michael had left it. The plan was just as Irish wished; Willa would be the star of the show and Michael would ensure she made curtain call.

But this morning both he and Willa had been useless. Willa forgot about the calendar. And he'd been so caught up in preparing for the afternoon appointment, Michael forgot to prompt Willa—even after Scot withheld Michael's first cup of coffee until he remembered his role in Irish's plan.

But when Willa got back to her house this morning and discovered Gabe's truck was gone and called Michael all in a tizzy, she actually *did* something her son suggested. She called Dr. Mac's office. The nice receptionist told her Gabe and Destiny had been there but had left about 15 minutes before.

Michael was relieved when he got the news from Willa that Gabe had in fact made the vet visit, but then Gabe phoned Michael. His brother-in-law spoke slowly. No, he wasn't calling to accept the evening's dinner invitation. He needed a favor. Could Destiny spend the night at their place? The fuel oil guy was a no-show, and The Castleton was freezing. If Michael or Scot weren't home when Gabe got there, he'd leave Dest in the backyard. He'd set a full bag of dog food at the back door. Before Michael could ask why a *full* bag of food for only one night, Gabe added, "Destiny's current on his shots." The phone had then gone dead.

Michael had gathered his thoughts before he dialed Willa. To keep it short, he suggested he just drive over to discuss with his parents the conversation he'd had with Gabe. Willa thought that was a fine idea, but again reminded her son not to say anything in front of his father about "the plan." No worries, Michael assured her.

"The plan," Michael knows, is the least of their concerns. Gabe is shutting down. Just like Irish had shared with her brother a year ago. Michael guesses he's known it all along but has been in denial as to the extent. Gabe's demeanor and tone on the phone this morning, if Michael had to describe it, sounded like a man beaten down to within an inch of his life. That isn't news he wants to share over the phone with his parents.

Michael barely stops the car in the driveway when Willa grabs the driver door handle. She struggles to open the door before he had a chance to shut off the engine, allowing the door to automatically unlock. Finally, Willa swings the door open and takes Michael's arm to hurry him out of the car. She is strangely silent. Then he sees his dad.

"Son, what a nice surprise! Scot send you over for a cup of flour for tonight's dinner?" Evan smiles at his own playful comment and hands Willa her plaid sweater he scooped up off the driveway.

"Mom and Dad, I think we have a problem."

## TWENTY-NINE

### GABE – Mommy Tummy Worm

Gabe parks in the cemetery lot next to the 'No Dogs Allowed' sign and lets Destiny out of the truck. The blacktop's covered with orange and yellow leaves from trees in harmony with the change of the season, shedding their foliage for winter.

Gabe follows Destiny to the lines of tombstones. He's trying to remember if it's the dog's first visit to the cemetery, but Destiny seems to know his way to the markers for Irish and Leesie. So far, the package tucked under Gabe's arm has gone undetected by the dog. But once Gabe catches up with Destiny, the dog jumps at his side until Gabe orders him to sit.

Standing between the two markers, Gabe looks to his right and whispers, "Hi, sweetheart. Happy Birthday." His eyes follow the engravings on the stone—the butterfly, his daughter's name, the date of her birth, the date of her death. He squats and runs his hand along the cold, slick stone. He's glad to see there are fresh flowers. Probably the mission Willa and

Evan were on this morning when they left their house. Gabe wishes he'd thought to bring flowers.

He looks to his left and sees an arrangement of fresh flowers identical to Leesie's. He hesitates. He doesn't know what to say to Irish. So much has happened already today, from delusions of hearing her and seeing her ghost, to discovering her actual handwriting, to the unexpected vet visit and then the quilt, not to mention the prison visit he has yet to make that afternoon.

Gabe slides the parcel out from under his arm and places it on the grass between the two gravestones. He stands and glances around to see if anyone is watching him. There is only a caretaker a ways off working near a concrete utility building. Gabe turns to leave when Destiny grabs the package between his teeth and takes off running with it.

Gabe sprints after the dog. Destiny runs in a straight line between two rows of head stones, and Gabe is gaining on him when the dog circles a maple tree, the parcel still dangling from his mouth.

"Mr. Hart, need some help?" It's the caretaker.

Gabe has no idea how the man knows his name, but he shouts back, no thanks. The 'No Dogs Allowed' sign flashes across his mind.

Gabe finally catches up with Destiny when the dog stops to drink from an ornate memorial fountain. With his front paws on the edge of the marble, the dog laps at the water while Gabe stands nearby slightly bent forward with his hands on his thighs, trying to catch his breath.

Destiny pushes off the edge of the fountain and shakes the excess water off his fur, then drags the package a short distance across the grass to where Gabe stands. Gabe sees the chase has been a rough one by the looks of the parcel. In an attempt to hang onto the oversized package, Destiny's teeth had torn a corner of the brown paper, exposing its contents.

Gabe goes to his knees not from exhaustion, but from the sight of little yellow butterflies.

He resists at first when Destiny nudges his hand toward the exposed quilt fabric. Gabe has sworn he'll never touch one stitch of that quilt. His hand, however, seems to float toward it, and his fingers trace the outline of a yellow butterfly. The flannel is soft. Gabe's eyes stream tears from the sensory memory.

◎ ◎ ◎

Leesie's butterfly pjs had been crazy too big for her the first time she wore them. The sleeves hung beyond her fingertips and the bottoms covered her feet. But she'd loved them just the way they were. Irish said she could exchange them the very next day and Leesie would have brand new ones that would fit her to a T. But Leesie gave a demonstration of how she liked that she could skate across the kitchen floor with her feet inside the pjs and flutter her arms like butterfly wings.

"Mrs. McPhillips taught us about caterpillars and butterflies in school. A caterpillar is kind of like a worm that grows into a butterfly. Daddy, was *I* ever like a worm?"

"Um, Irish … ." Gabe began, but Irish waved goodbye over her shoulder as she closed the back kitchen door.

"Well, Leesie, yes, guess you could say you were *like* a worm."

"Did I hang upside down under a leaf?"

"No, sweetie, you grew inside Mommy's tummy."

"How did I get like a worm inside Mommy's tummy?"

"Whoa, careful there! You almost flew into the refrigerator."

He'd crossed the room and started randomly opening cabinets, making as much noise as he could with no purpose other than to divert his daughter's line of questioning.

"So, I thought we'd go to the store today and buy a kite. We can go over to Fallow Ridge Park. Sound like fun?"

"Can we get a butterfly kite?"

"Yes, if they have one, we'll definitely get a butterfly kite."

"Do they have caterpillar kites?"

"Leesie, I don't know, but I doubt it. We'll look though."

"Do they have mommy tummy worm kites?"

He scooped Leesie into his arms. "I'll tell ya what. If they have mommy tummy worm kites, I'll buy 10!"

After lunch, Gabe and Leesie went in search of a kite.

"Hi, Mr. Arnold!" Leesie ran up to the hardware store owner. "We need 10 mommy tummy worm kites!"

"Why, hello, Leesie Hart! Well, wouldn't you know, we're fresh out of those. How about this nice dragonfly kite? Or this monarch butterfly one?"

"Thank you, Mr. Arnold. We'll take the butterfly. Okay, Daddy?"

Extra string and packaged butterfly kite in hand, Leesie stopped at the door and called back, "Mr. Arnold? Will you please let Daddy know when you have mommy tummy worm kites? He would like to buy 10. He told me *all* about mommy tummy worms."

Gabe found it hard to look at Mr. Arnold with a straight face.

*Mommy tummy worms.* So typical Leesie.

◉ ◉ ◉

"Excuse me, Mr. Hart?"

Gabe lifts his head to find the caretaker towering over him. The lean figure wears soiled gloves with the fingertips cut off. He holds in one hand a folded piece of white paper.

Gabe stands. "I'm sorry. I know I'm not supposed to have my dog here … ." Gabe hopes the paper is a warning and not a fine.

"Oh, I didn't come to trouble you none about that, Mr. Hart." The caretaker hands Gabe the paper. "This dropped out of the package the dog was running with. Hey, that wouldn't be Destiny would it?"

"Why, yes, it is."

Destiny hears his name and sits by the caretaker for a pet.

"I'm William." The caretaker removes his ball cap exposing a full head of hair. Gabe expects the young man wants to shake hands, but instead the dog gets a pat on the head. "I never did get a chance to tell you how sorry I was to hear about Mrs. Hart."

"Thanks, William. You knew my wife?" Gabe stuffs the quilt package under his arm and fidgets with the folded piece of paper in his hand.

"No, sir, I didn't know her 'cept sometimes she'd come here by herself. I'd help her get a bouquet out of the car sometimes. And just kind of watch out for her was all. She mentioned your little girl had had a dog named Destiny. Nice dog."

"Yea, but he can be handful." Gabe shifts his stance and struggles to think of something to say. "You keep everything looking great around here."

"Well, I didn't mean to bother you none, Mr. Hart." William pushes back his hair and slips on his ball cap. "If there's anything I can do, just let me know. Reckon I'll see you next year." As the caretaker turns to go, his eyes meet Gabe's, and he adds, "If not before."

# THIRTY

## MICHAEL – The Huddle

Michael suggests they all go into the kitchen, but his parents are anxious to hear about the problem. The three huddle in the driveway where the noon sun offers at least some warmth. Willa hugs her plaid sweater and Evan leans in while Michael relays Gabe's side of the phone conversation.

Careful not to divulge Irish and Willa's precious "plan," Michael shares that his sister confided in him before she passed that within a year she feared her husband would go into complete shutdown mode. And from what Michael can tell with Gabe asking for Destiny to spend the night and leaving a full bag of dogfood, he is doing exactly that.

Yes, his parents agree, Gabe is not the same man they once knew. He pulls away from them more and more every day. They share with Michael how they're trying to figure out how to best approach their son-in-law, so that he doesn't think they are just two needy old people.

Evan relays to Michael that Gabe hasn't been in the utility garage for a couple of years. But last night, when Evan got up to use the restroom, he noticed the garage light was on. Evan happened to see Gabe exit the garage before dawn and was back out there this morning when he and Willa were heading out.

Michael nods when Evan asks him if he remembers the Leesie memory quilt Irish had made. Michael notices his mother seems surprised when Evan shares that after delivering it to Gabe that morning, he'd adamantly refused it, but then grabbed the package and tossed it on a stack of newspapers just inside the utility garage door.

Evan saves the most troubling detail for last. He'd been hit with heavy exhaust fumes when his son-in-law opened the small garage door to greet him that morning. Evan said he'd told Gabe he should have had the big garage door open for ventilation. Why, something like that could kill a person, Evan says.

Willa cuts in asking, "Oh, my! Was that what Gabe tried to do? Kill himself?" She adds, "Do we know if Gabe has a *gun?*"

Evan rubs his chin and mentions a woman he'd heard collected sleeping pills over the course of a year to end her life. Actually, hadn't Cooder Ward done the same thing? He'd not been successful, of course.

Michael believes the situation could be grave but he needs to remain calm for his parents. He tells Willa and Evan he appreciates their gun and pills theories, but they should stay focused on what Evan said about Gabe being in the garage most of the night and the exhaust fumes.

Without a word between them, all three walk to Gabe's garage. Michael tests the big garage door which is locked just like the small side door.

Michael sees the worry on Willa and Evan's faces and tried to calm them further by saying they're all probably over-reacting. In his heart, however, he suspects they're not far from the truth—that Gabe is dangerously near the end of his rope.

Michael suggests that his mom and dad wait inside their house while he goes home to confront Gabe when he drops off Destiny. The first one to see Gabe will phone the other.

Michael has turned his car halfway around in the driveway when Willa again flags him down. He lowers the driver window.

"Michael! Michael!" She grabs the car door where the window had receded and pokes her head through the opening. "What if you get home and Gabe's already left Destiny there and he never shows up here?"

# THIRTY-ONE

## GABE – A Brief Blessing

When Gabe calls Michael, he mentions he has an important meeting at 1 o'clock. Gabe knows Scot usually hits the grocery after the lunch crowd, so he'll most likely be shopping for that night's dinner at 1 o'clock. It's settled. Gabe will wait until 1 p.m, just to make sure the guys aren't home when he drops off Destiny. He's in no mood for a pop quiz about why he hasn't ordered fuel oil or why he can't come for dinner or stay the night with Destiny.

Gabe considers where he might go to kill time until he heads to Michael and Scot's. The park at Fallow Ridge is about the right distance and should be empty—most adults work on a Tuesday and kids are in school. It'll be good to be somewhere alone.

Inside the park, Gabe climbs out of the truck and pats his thigh for Destiny to follow. He finds a clean bench and pulls the note out of his jacket pocket. He has no idea what the paper contains other than it was inside the quilt package. Never wanting anything to do with the quilt, he considers chucking the note in one of the park trash containers. But what if it's one of Leesie's drawings? He pictures mounds of rotten banana peels, chewed apple cores, sticky drink bottles, and greasy fried chicken dumped on top of the paper in the trash container, and his stomach turns.

He glances up to check on Destiny, who is near the shelter house rolling on his back in a pile of leaves. Unfolding the paper, Gabe notices a finger smudge. Must have come from William, the caretaker. Then he sees Irish's handwriting.

My dearest Gabe,

How I wonder where you'll be when you read this. For some reason, I'm picturing you at our kitchen table.

I wonder, too, where I will be. I have no idea, and that scares me a little,

Oh, Gabe, I will miss you with more than all my heart. I already do. I miss how your arms held me when you didn't worry that you might break me in two.

We were a team, Gabriel Hart. You and me. I'm the luckiest girl in the world to have been loved by you. Did you know, even before our first date, I practiced writing Irish E. Hart inside my school notebook? I don't think I ever told you.

You were, no, you are the love of my life. And when you read this, I hope you'll know that even though my life is over, my love lives on. I will be with you at our bedside. I will be with you at the gravesite. I will be with you at the prison.

As I write these words, you've yet to promise, but I trust as you read this you'll soon be on your way to see Cooder Ward, if you've not already.

Yes, I asked you to make me that promise for purely selfish reasons. I imagine you're angry and resentful.

Gabe, my love, what if you were in my place? Would you let hate destroy me? You couldn't bear that any more than I can.

Thank you, my angel Gabriel, for loving our daughter and me with all of your heart.

Your Irish, always

PS Oh, Gabe, a memory I kept having as I made the quilt was Mommy Tummy Worms! Remember? Leesie was our butterfly, our beautiful, brief blessing.

Gabe rereads Irish's letter even when tears make seeing the words impossible .

## Thirty-Two

### GABE – Twice in One Day

Gabe pulls into Sulley's for a second time that day, but this trip he tops off the tank. He'll need it for the prison drive.

Wendel smiles from behind the cash register. "Twice in one day, eh?"

"Yeah, got extra errands I hadn't planned on."

"I was in the back, but saw you pull out earlier. Hey, reminds me. Had someone come around asking about you not 10 minutes after you left the last time. Clean-cut fella, least that's what the new guy Barney said. In a blue Volvo, I think he said. Yeah, that's what it was. Naturally Barney didn't tell him anything. Didn't have nothing to tell!" Wendel wipes his hands on a grimy rag and steps from behind the counter. "Listen, know who it might have been? That friend of yours who moved away. What's his name?"

"Jon. Jon Elam." Gabe spots duct tape on a wall display to his right. He drops two large rolls on the counter. "How much? Ten enough?"

"He's a nice guy." Wendel rings up the sale. "This is extra heavy duty tape. Sure you want this? We've got regular duct next to it."

"This is fine."

"Well, it's a shame he had to move, that Jon fella. He lived right next to you. See him much?"

"Not really. Listen, Wendel, I'm in kind of a hurry." Gabe feels bad for brushing Wendel off, so adds jokingly, "Maybe I'll have more time if I stop in again today."

"Ha, that's a good one, Gabe! Haven't seen the ole balloon chase van in here for a while. Maybe stop by and fill *it* up, eh?"

"Yeah, maybe." Gabe is taken aback that Wendel should mention the van. Gabe was getting the tape because he seems to remember one of the van windows doesn't quite close all the way. Plus, he can use the tape to make sure the rag is secure in the van's tail pipe.

◉ ◉ ◉

Gabe is also taken aback that Wendel mentioned Jon. It's like at every turn today Jon is there. Or calling or something. He's like an albatross around Gabe's neck.

Driving to Michael and Scot's, Gabe shakes his head recalling how Jon and Irish had cooked up the whole eye donation thing. Well, in reality it was Irish's idea, but Jon hadn't tried to stop her. He'd been her accomplice. Together they orchestrated the whole awful thing.

Gabe sure as hell never asked Irish anything about the corneal donation or Jon's specific participation. Now he wonders if Irish went so far as to tell Jon about the promise Gabe needs to keep.

Gabe turns onto Michael and Scot's street. No sign of their cars parked at the curb or in the driveway.

He needs to make this quick before either of the guys returns home. Gabe doesn't know how many more times he can tell Destiny goodbye before he changes his mind about the whole thing.

After several tries, pulling out clay dishes from under pots of mums, Gabe finds one without a hole in the bottom. He turns on the garden hose and rinses out the dish before filling it with water. Destiny laps at the fresh water while Gabe quickly sets the bag of dog food beside the back door, double-checks the gate lock on the chain link fence around the backyard and jumps back into the truck.

Gabe speeds away without looking back, wiping his eyes with a sleeve cuff.

◉ ◉ ◉

The visitor parking lot at Harper Correctional Facility is almost empty. Gabe pulls the truck into an end space, climbs out, and walks toward the prison entrance. Looking up at the double rolls of concertina wire atop the prison walls, he steps off the curb into the path of a small bus transporting guards.

The bus driver swerves to avoid striking Gabe. Gabe's heart races. It flashes through his mind that maybe Jon was right. Leesie's small body never stood a chance against a ton of iron and steel.

# THIRTY-THREE

## JON – They Steal Your Heart Away

Jon parks his blue Volvo near the cemetery gate. He carefully removes from the backseat two identical sunflower arrangements he purchased at Smith's Florist. Turning to see the line upon line of headstones, he's momentarily overwhelmed. He'd forgotten how huge the cemetery is and only hopes he can find Irish and Leesie's graves. He needn't have worried. He walks right to them, as though following in his own footprints from a year ago. Both graves, however, already have stunning sprays of fresh spider mums. Suddenly he doesn't want to raise questions about who would bring sunflowers, so he places them in front of two nearby headstones.

Jon paces anxiously between the two graves recalling the morning's encounter with Cooder Ward and then seeing Gabe pulled off the side of the road in the exact spot where dear Leesie had died.

He needs to clear his thoughts and sets out to walk a bit. He heads toward a decorative marble fountain. He notices how immaculate the cemetery grounds are when he spots a piece of brown wrapping paper littering the grass. He picks it up and sticks it in a pocket.

Just beyond the fountain he pauses by a small pond that reminds him of Leesie's balloon ride, and Gabe radioing the chase crew, "Splash and dash!" Jon could only imagine Leesie's excitement when the bottom of the wicker basket touched the water's surface.

From the backseat of the chase van that day, Jon had studied Irish riding shotgun because he expected to see her smiling knowing what a thrill it was for her daughter to take her first balloon ride. But Irish had been chewing her thumbnail.

Jon hadn't a clue why Irish was nervous until Tom positioned the chase van in the open field and they all spotted electric lines. As the three of them jumped from the van and ran to catch the balloon basket, Jon knew why Irish hadn't been excited about the Echo Pond adventure. She'd sensed something was about to happen. She had a gift of premonition, except the morning Leesie died.

From where he stands beside the small cemetery pond, Jon sees a stone bench and heads straight for it; his legs suddenly feeling weak. He'd previously had no appetite for breakfast or lunch, but now has a hollow, empty feeling in the pit of his stomach. He should have eaten something instead of drinking three cups of coffee.

Only a few feet from where he sits towers the statue of an angel with a gentle smile and open arms. His hope has always been that after Leesie died in his arms, a sweet angel had gently carried her to the other side. Never before had Jon heard someone's dying words or seen what he thought was someone's soul rise above their body.

Before the moment Leesie died, he'd been just a guy who loved touch football, Christmas morning, nonfiction books about World War I and

II, red wine and Italian food, his parents, his bride, his best friend and his wife, and his goddaughter. The last three were no longer a part of Jon's life, and he was at a loss as what to do about it.

Sandy had suggested he try grief counseling after Leesie died. He refused. She mentioned the idea again after they moved away, and once more after Irish died. Still, he said no. The Grief Center was amazing, Sandy said, and they had a team of wonderful counselors so Jon wouldn't have to talk to the same one she had seen. She even promised not to ask questions about his sessions.

Jon looks out over the sea of headstones and wonders how many of the deceased have loved ones as wise as his wife or as stubborn as her husband.

Irish, for one, had a pig-headed husband. Gabe has refused to talk to Jon the last three years. He wonders if Gabe has permanently blocked Jon's number or just declined his calls every time he phones. Jon's even tried reaching out at different times of the day to try and catch his best friend.

"One day he'll be ready to hear it," Irish had said during her office visit. Jon isn't remotely convinced.

A young man pushing a wheelbarrow approaches Jon where he sits on the bench. "Afternoon," the young man says, tipping his soiled ball cap. "The tallest monument in the cemetery," he adds setting down the wheelbarrow, freeing his hands to shield his eyes from the sun as he looks into the angel's face. The young man is obviously the groundskeeper and yet he looks as if he were seeing the angel for the first time. "Sorry," he says, grabbing the wheelbarrow's handles. "Didn't mean to bother you none."

"No, no bother. No bother at all," Jon assures him. But the caretaker moves on, and, curious as to where he might be going with the wheelbarrow, Jon watches him until the young man seems to vanish from view. Jon looks again into the angel's benevolent face.

On the surface, the encounter with the groundskeeper seems insignificant. But in thinking about it, isn't that how Jon's been treating his relationship with Gabe? As though he doesn't want to be a bother? Or that it isn't all that important they connect? Sure, he calls Gabe all the time, unsuccessfully. And he drove by the house, but has he tried to do more? My God, he thinks, he's my *best friend!*

That settles it. Jon will talk to Gabe today, if it is the last thing he does.

He hadn't come to the cemetery to gain clarity regarding what to do about Gabe—but he is grateful for the unexpected insight.

He came to the cemetery to find the strength to go back to the prison. Irish would have done so if it were her. She'd go right back and apologize to Cooder Ward for having such an emotional outburst during the eye exam. Jon had been totally unprofessional. But even more, and crazy as it seems, because Cooder Ward had Irish's corneas, Jon feels like Irish saw him verbally attack a patient.

Jon returns to the random headstones where he'd placed the sunflowers, removes both arrangements and sets one at his goddaughter's gravesite. The other he places near the engraving. "When Irish eyes are smiling, sure, they steal your heart away."

## THIRTY-FOUR

### THE GUARD – Window Four

The guard grabs the back of the seat in front of him as the bus swerves to keep from hitting a man stepping off the curb into traffic. Fool, he thinks, pushing his thick glasses up on his nose.

Inside the facility, he pulls his timecard and punches in, then smooths his uniform and examines his firearm before heading to the visiting area. Today he's assigned to the visitors' side of the room. He prefers that to the building's entrance or the other side of the glass with the prisoners. His wife jokes he likes being with the visitors because he can eavesdrop on what they were saying. He can't deny there's some appeal to hearing what folks from the outside say to those on the inside.

Scarcely a minute after he takes his station, the first visitor to walk through the door is the man who stepped in front of the bus. The guard asks to see the man's wristband, but the man seems confused as to which arm it's on. The guard has to hold the man's wrist steady until he verbally confirms the visitor's name, date of birth, and last four digits of his

Social. The man stumbles on his Social, but finally gets the numbers in the correct sequence, then stands staring at the wall of glass divided by metal partitions.

"Where do I go?" the man asks.

The guard points to the large plastic card the man's holding. Even without his thick glasses, the guard thinks, he can't miss the huge number on the card. "Window 4."

The guard wonders if the man is possibly on drugs, then decides he is acting more sleep deprived than anything. But there's something else about the man that gives the guard pause, something he's seen in many a troubled man's eyes. He has the look of someone who thinks they have nothing left to lose.

The guard will keep an eye on Window Four.

# THIRTY-FIVE

## JON – The Badge

Jon unintentionally parks beside Gabe's truck in the prison parking lot. Okay, he thinks, this isn't quite the way he imagined everything playing out when he left the cemetery. Fortunately, Gabe's not in the truck, just two rolls of heavy-duty duct tape on the passenger seat. Jon walks around the back bumper to get a closer look at a torn, rumpled package with brown wrapping paper he spotted in the truck bed. He removes the piece of wrapping from his jacket pocket and confirms it's from the package. So, Gabe was at the cemetery earlier in the day.

The visitor parking lot, Jon notes, is even less inviting than the covered staff garage. He has to cross the street at one designated place and stay left of the bus lane.

Inside the prison, Jon looks closely at the guards to see if he recognizes anyone from the morning. It's unlikely he'll run into the same guards given that earlier today he was in the medical wing of the prison. Jon knows his behavior was so unprofessional that he fears if the warden gets wind that

Jon's returned, it might not go very well. Jon just hopes his name isn't at the top of a no admittance list.

A guard confirms Dr. Jon Elam is on Cooder Ward's list of approved visitors and instructs him to slip off his shoes and empty his pockets before walking through the metal detector. At the registration desk, Jon's informed Cooder Ward already has a visitor. Does he want to wait? *Want to wait?* No, Jon thinks. What he wants to do is climb back in his Volvo and drive off Fallow Ridge. Not really, but wonders if Gabe ever considers such a thing.

Jon pushes up his jacket cuff while a fat plastic band containing his personal information is snapped around his wrist. He's told, however, he wouldn't be issued a card pass until the prisoner is ready for his next visitor. He's directed to a wait in a stuffy, narrow windowless hall the size of a storage closet. There are a couple of beat up chairs, but he's too anxious to sit. He nervously unzips his jacket.

Eventually, he looks around a corner and sees a door marked Restricted Area–Authorized Visitors Only. He nods at a guard bursting through the door carrying a stack of plastic cards. The guard's footsteps stop. "Excuse me," the guard says.

The jig's up, Jon thinks. He's been recognized. Jon turns, an apology waiting on his lips—he's sorry; he should have let the warden know he wanted to see Cooder Ward a second time, and he promises not to make a scene, if only—but the guard merely points to the physician's badge dangling from a lanyard around Jon's neck. Jon looks down at his chest trying not to appear surprised at seeing the badge.

The guard asks if the doctor is familiar with security procedures. He just needs to hold the badge up to the sensor to enter the restricted visitor area; he doesn't need a numbered pass, like the ones the guard has in his hand. Thanks, Jon says, he's been waiting for a pass. Good to know, he says, and thanks the guard.

The guard continues down the hall, and Jon says thank you again, this time silently for not having been ceremoniously escorted from the prison or, worse yet, to the warden's office.

So, apparently in his haste to leave the prison that morning, he'd failed to surrender his badge. And he guesses he hadn't unzipped his jacket all day until minutes ago in the waiting room.

The badge changes everything. He has access to the visitor area right now. He doesn't have to wait for Gabe to leave. But he's come to see Cooder Ward, not Gabe. Does he even want to see Gabe under these conditions? No, not really. He'd rather wait until later today, maybe try stopping by the house again around five or so.

The badge is only good for today, and a guard said he'll need to get another wristband tomorrow, if for some reason the prisoner is not permitted a second visitor today. Jon wishes he'd asked for an example or two of "some reason."

But maybe his decision has already been made for him. He knows the badge is only good for today, but maybe he isn't authorized to enter the visitor area, only the medical floor he'd been assigned.

Jon approaches the door and holds the badge against the sensor. The red penlight doesn't so much as flicker. He has his answer. He doesn't have access to the visitor area regardless of what the guard with the passes told him. And after all, the warden had been very clear just this morning that "a strict regimen is the cornerstone of our correctional facility."

Jon notices, however, his palms are sweaty, like they were in the morning when he arrived at the prison, so he dries his hands and the badge on his jacket and tries again. The light flashes green, and the heavy metal door swooshes opened automatically.

## THIRTY-SIX

### GABE – Tall Weeds Wet with Dew

The institution-grade fluorescents and the harsh light they cast on the prison visitor area momentarily transports Gabe to the sleeping dorm in one of the orphanages of his youth. He'd climbed out of the toddler-sized bed at night, because he could, flipped on the lights, because he liked to, and roamed the tile floor in his bare feet. He'd peek through vertical slats at sleeping babies who occupied the row of cribs along a wall of interior glass windows. A large woman wearing blue pants and a bunny-print top would scoop him up and tuck him back in the toddler bed. She'd pat his head and whisper "sweet dreams." He'd ask her to please leave the lights on. But she never did.

In the dark cavernous room full of sleeping children, the memories would begin. Gabe's little head slamming against the back of the padded car seat. His dad shouting, "Staaaay—wiiiith— meeeee—Esssss—ther." His dad's heavy panting as he carried Gabe strapped in his car seat and placed him in tall weeds wet with dew. Gabe's daddy running back across the pavement the way he'd come, a shadow against a bank of headlights. Gabe's small hands releasing his ears when the sound of shrill horns and screaming voices suddenly fell silent like they were sucked out of the air, and all he heard was the thump, thump inside his chest.

The explosion rocked his car seat. His eyes followed the ball of fire shooting into the dark sky. He thought he saw his mother's face in a billow of smoke. "Momma!" he cried. A man ran up to him and asked if he was okay. "Momma!"

Gabe shakes off the childhood memory and looks around at the line of gray chairs to his right and left and drops down onto the one at Window Four. He tries to scoot the chair back for more legroom, but all of the chair legs were bolted to the floor. He guesses the chairs were that way so visitors couldn't pick them up and throw them through the glass partitions, hoping to attack prisoners on the other side, or bash other visitors in the head. God, he doesn't want to be here.

He reaches into his jeans pocket and pulls out the plastic bag containing the shamrock pin. Irish once suggested he bring for luck. He removes the shamrock shape from the bag. Yeah, luck. That's rich.

Rubbing the pin between his fingers, for some reason, triggers an idea. He can leave the prison right now on a technicality. After all, he *is* here, just like he promised Irish. The prisoner hasn't shown yet, which isn't Gabe's fault. Gabe *could* just leave.

Who is he kidding? He has to look the prisoner right in the eyes, *that's* what he promised Irish.

He wishes his legs would stop that juddery thing they've started doing lately when he's anxious. He flips the shamrock onto the shelf in front of him and rubs his hands along his thighs. He needs to get on with it. What the hell does a prisoner have to do so important he keeps a visitor waiting?

He glances at the wall clock and back down at his thighs. It's already 3:30 p.m. He has to be back home by 5 o'clock.

The guard who had admitted Gabe to the visitor area circles behind him. It seems to Gabe he's being watched excessively. Then again he *is* the only visitor in the area.

"Go ahead. You can pick up the phone now."

Gabe jumps at the sound of the guard's deep voice. Luckily he looks up just enough to see the shamrock on the shelf and catch a glimpse of the orange jumpsuit across from him on the other side of the glass.

He's sickened at the thought of having to look into the prisoner's face, let alone before it's absolutely necessary. Gabe keeps his focus on the shiny green shamrock while he fumbles for the receiver. He presses it to his ear and the guard retreats.

Gabe closes his eyes. He hears muffled voices across the room as the guard admits a new visitor. Through the phone receiver, however, the only sound is Gabe's own breath. He repositions the mouthpiece under his chin, so he doesn't have to hear himself breathe.

Now, however, he hears through the earpiece quick, anxious breaths originating from the prisoner. Gabe's face burns like he's standing dangerously close to a propane flame. *Irish, I can't do this.* Breathing and more incessant breathing bombards his brain. He wants to slam the earpiece down on the shelf in front of him.

"God, just stop *breathing*." He's surprised to hear himself speak, but his voice was low and steady. He's in control.

And then he wasn't. Suddenly he can't stop his words any more than the prisoner's breath. "Do *not* take another breath. Ever. God, just stop. End it all right now. Not that difficult. Just do yourself in and *stop breathing*. Prisoners do it all the time."

There. He's said what he's wanted to say for three years. He opens his eyes and focuses on his fist resting near the shamrock. Nothing left to lose. "Hell, don't do it. Don't end it all, and just see who's waiting for your sorry ass if you ever walk out those prison gates." Gabe knows it's an irrational threat, given his plan to end it all, but who knows, maybe it will scare the prisoner into ending his own life.

Gabe can't believe how easily he's been able to spill his guts once he got started. Maybe he should have made this visit *months* ago.

Gabe stretches his field of vision beyond his fist and the shamrock to include the narrow shelf on the opposite side of the glass. It appears freshly sanded and painted compared to the

ledge in front of Gabe. Gripping the shelf on the prisoner's side of the partition is a trembling hand with fingernails chewed to the quick.

The same killer's hand that took his little girl's life. The hand that murdered her the same as if it strangled her neck. The reckless hand that once held a steering wheel but didn't swerve fast enough. The hand that threw an empty gin bottle out of the car window, that became evidence against the driver, not 200 feet from where the little girl lay fallen, in pain, dying on the side of the road.

God, Irish, is *this* what you wanted? Is *this* why you made me promise to sit across from this piece of crap? To put *me* through this hell?

Gabe rocks. He's ready. He needs to go home and seal up the garage and start the van and be done with it all. Finish this now, Gabe.

"Look, who the hell knows what Irish was thinking when she donated her eyes to *you*. But I do know this. She used you. Used you to get to me. She wanted *me* to stop grieving, to get on with my life. Not to save your frigging eyesight." Gabe's voice begins to elevate. "You *murdered* our little girl. You don't deserve to see. You don't deserve to *live*."

Out of the corner of his eye, Gabe sees the guard approaching him. Gabe gives the guard a thumbs-up indicating he will keep his voice down. God, a minute ago, he couldn't wait to run out of this place. Now, Gabe can't chance getting thrown out. He isn't near done.

"Listen," he begins, eyes intent on the shamrock that lay between him and the prisoner, "the minute you get back to your cell, do it. Just do it. Take those miserable hands that killed my daughter and do the right thing. *Kill* yourself."

*Kill* yourself. Yes, he knows he's talking to himself as well as the prisoner. Gabe's head begins pounding. He's having trouble focusing his gaze or attention.

Words begin spilling from his lips.

"You ... *you* know what you did that morning, what you did was wrong ... right?" Gabe shakes his head. "Oh, I know, I know you ... you probably thought, it'll be fine. I ... I can manage."

Gabe isn't sure if he's even talking to the *prisoner* anymore. Sweat beads on his forehead. He's barely able to catch his breath. Suddenly he's lost in the memory of Leesie the last time he saw her alive. She was sitting on the bottom porch step, chin in her hands, admiring her beautiful new bike, promising to wait until her parents came back out before riding it anywhere but near the utility garage.

Of course. Leesie'd thought it would all be fine. She'd just ride a little bit beyond the utility garage. She had no idea something *awful* would happen. All she wanted was to ride her shiny new bike.

Gabe closes his eyelids and presses the fingers of his free hand hard against them.

Probably before she knew it, she'd ventured farther and farther down the driveway. She likely thought she'd be back up the driveway before he and Irish came outside again. Even if we found out she'd ridden to the end of the driveway, she probably figured it *was* her birthday, and we'd forgive her that once. She must have thought she'd never be missed. She never planned … .

Gabe opens his eyes to see a tear fall on the back of the prisoner's hand before the hand slides out of view.

"You're *crying?* What the hell? You got Irish's eyes, but *you* don't get to shed her tears."

"Mr. Hart." The prisoner's voice startles Gabe. "Yes, sir, I, I do know what I did was wrong. And I did try to do myself in, just like you said. But Mrs. Hart, well, she gave me her eyes. I knew why she'd done it. So you'd come."

"Oh, doesn't that make *you* special." Gabe chokes back bile. "You think *you're* the reason I'm here? Trust me. You're not why I'm here. I'm here because I made a promise to my wife. *Irish* is why I'm sitting here."

"I, I know, Mr. Hart. I made Mrs. Hart a promise, too. Why I'm still here."

"Who the hell cares why *you're* still here?" Gabe's head is spinning. "And what does a *promise* mean anyway?"

Leesie had promised him, and she was no longer here. *I promise, Daddy, I'll wait.* She'd promised not to ride her bike until Mommy or Daddy were outside with her.

"Leesie," Gabe unknowingly whispers aloud his thoughts, "why didn't you keep your promise to me, sweetie? I had no way to protect you."

"Gabe." The voice did not come through the phone this time, but rather from over Gabe's shoulder. He spins around in the chair and sees Jon Elam standing only a few feet away. "Leesie didn't want you to be mad at her."

Gabe's trapped. God, he wanted to run. He has the prisoner on one side, acting like some damn *expert*, telling Gabe what his own wife thought and planned, and Jon on the other side of him with the nerve to tell Gabe what was deepest in his dying daughter's heart.

Gabe glares at Jon, then looks away. "Of course, I'm not *mad at her!*"

But the truth was, Gabe realizes, he is desperately angry at Leesie.

God, he wishes he could throw the damn chair.

"Gabe, I know you don't want to hear Leesie's last words," Jon inches a bit closer to Gabe, "but you have to. You need to."

The receiver springs out of Gabe's hand when he lunges out of the chair toward Jon. The guard is on Gabe in an instant grabbing his shoulders.

Jon continues. "Leesie said, 'Please tell Daddy I'm sorry.'"

Gabe pulls himself from the guard's hold and collapses onto the chair, hands on his juddering knees, eyes on his hands.

Jon and the guard speak to each other in low voices, but Gabe doesn't care what they're saying. He's trying to imagine Leesie those final moments. Had she been gasping or crying out in pain when she said she was sorry? Had she spoken so low that Jon could have mistaken what she said? Or was Jon just trying to make a point with Gabe? That, he knows, isn't fair. That isn't who Jon ever was or could be.

"You best mind yourself." The guard towers over Gabe.

"Yes, sir," Gabe manages to utter. "I'm sorry. Won't happen again."

"You got *that* right, Window Four. Sorry don't mean crap here. Dr. Elam vouched for you. Otherwise, I'd throw your ass the hell out of here."

Gabe nods and gropes for the receiver, and closes his eyes.

How could Leesie's final words be that *she* was sorry? *He* was the one who was sorry. He was sorry he never told Irish the truth, that every morning he had to face in the mirror the man responsible for their daughter's death.

*He* was the one who pushed to let Leesie ride her bike that morning. *He* was the one who thought there'd be freezing rain later in the day and wanted Leesie to have a chance to get a bike ride in beforehand, before the school bus arrived. It was *he* who decided to catch a quick shower before Leesie's bike ride when he knew Irish was starting laundry in the basement. He honestly thought there'd be plenty of time. Leesie would gather her school stuff, they'd all meet outside, and she'd ride her bike for the first time. It was supposed to be a perfect start to Leesie's ninth birthday.

But Leesie hadn't gathered her books. She hadn't waited for her daddy. And she hadn't stayed in the driveway on the hill.

For three years he's been angry. Mad at himself, mad at Irish, mad at anyone responsible for them living on that curve. And mad at Leesie.

Now, having admitted it for the first time, he hates himself for ever being angry at Leesie. And learning how sorry Leesie had been, he can't bear to think about his little girl feeling guilty and worrying about *her daddy* while she lay dying.

Gabe ached from his chest to his backbone thinking how, for God's sake, she was worrying about *him* with her last breath. Did she *know* she was dying? Did she know she'd never see him again? Or Irish? Or Destiny? Did Jon brush back her curls and tell her everything would be okay?

Oh Leesie, he thought, you were pure joy, pure innocence. I wish angels did exist so they could have greeted you and assured her how much your daddy loves you. Oh, sweetheart, you were the most precious daughter from here to the moon and back, and please, please know how much I love you, and don't ever worry again, ever, it wasn't your fault, I know you were sorry, but there's nothing to forgive, spunky-doodle. I should have been there. But if maybe you need to hear me say it, okay, of course, I will, and I'm sorry it's been such a long time coming, I was stubborn and should have listened to Uncle Jon three years ago, but yes, yes, of course, Leesie, always. "I forgive you."

*God, did I say that aloud? Into the phone? To the prisoner?*

No, no, no. He has to see if the prisoner heard him, but he isn't ready. He *has* to remember his wife the way she was. The way her eyes smiled. How they bathed Leesie, him, Destiny, everyone, with love. How they danced with mischief from time to time. How they always seemed to see things coming long before Gabe ever did.

But he promised Irish. And time is running out …

Torn between guilt and the need to keep his word, Gabe opens his eyes and raises his gaze. Through the smugged, thick glass, where previous prisoners and visitors had exchanged news, good and bad, glances, happy and sad, some touching it with their hands from either side—Gabe sees an empty gray chair.

# THIRTY-SEVEN

## GABE – Something Left to Lose

Gabe looks over his shoulder and breathes a sigh of relief to see Jon has already left the visitor area. The guard approaches Gabe at the exit.

"None of my business," the guard says, pushing up his glasses, "but I never met a prisoner more sorry for what he done than that one. And after 25 years, I've seen it all, including visitors not satisfied with the justice system. Wanting to take matters into their own hands. Telling a prisoner how he should save up sleeping pills and take a handful or rip his bed sheets into strips to hang himself." The guard, who was the same height as Gabe, peers over the top of his thick glasses. "I'm a fair judge of people, Window Four. You seem like a logical man. The law's the law for a reason. It's against the law—suicide. A lot of people don't know that. Sure, life's hard, and people think they'd got nothing left to lose, right, Window Four? But everybody, *everybody's* got *something* left to lose."

◉ ◉ ◉

Making his way to the parking lot, Gabe's head is splitting and his legs can barely carry him. When he finally makes it to the truck, Gabe holds onto door handle to steady himself. He thought the whole motivation for him coming today, the *whole* reason behind his promise to Irish had been to look into Cooder Ward's eyes. Not an empty gray chair.

*Now* what is he supposed to do? He can't go back into that prison. It's already 3:45. And clearly he can't come back tomorrow.

And what was up with that mini sermon from the guard? The officer doesn't know Gabe from Adam. What gave him the right to call Gabe "Window Four," and what was he getting at with "everybody's got *something* left to lose?"

Before Gabe climbs into the driver's seat, he glances in the truck bed. Tucked under the string tied around the soft brown package with various rips and tears was a torn piece of the same wrapping.

Gabe notices the familiar blue Volvo parked next to the truck.

Speeding from of the parking lot, Gabe looks in the rearview mirror half-hoping to see the torn piece of wrapping paper fly into the air.

# THIRTY-EIGHT

## GABE – The Barn Owl

Gabe swings into Sulley's for the third time in six hours. Wendel is inside cleaning grease off his hands with the same soiled rag Gabe noticed from an earlier visit.

"You going for a record today? Need to give you a a free fill up for a prize! Anyway, what can I do you for, Gabe?"

Gabe hands Wendel the unopened rolls of duct tape purchased during the last visit. "Wonder could I trade these out, Wendel? Didn't open them."

"Sure, Gabe. What ya need?"

"Got a tow strap?"

"Sure thing. How long do you need it? Ha! Guess you need it for a long time. I meant to ask what length tow strap ya looking for?"

Gabe picks out a strap. They settle up the sale, and as Gabe waves over his shoulder Wendel calls to him, "Hey, need me to keep the station open late tonight in case you think of something else?"

◉ ◉ ◉

Gabe's sure he'll remember how to get to the abandoned barn. He drove there alone during the trial to see where the police found Leesie's murderer.

There'd been yellow crime scene tape everywhere, just like the kind that'd been strung in front of their house for a week or more.

He turns onto a dirt road and follows it for about a half a mile. He spots the barn's ramshackle roof in the middle of the deserted cornfield and aims the truck's tires for the wheel ruts leading that direction.

He drives right into the barn and parks the truck perpendicular to what appears to be a sturdy rafter, positioning the truck cab directly beneath it. He turns off the engine and removes the yellow tow strap from the packaging.

He rolls down the driver window and opens the door, then steps up on the seat and throws the tow strap on the top of the truck cab. He lifts his left leg and places his foot on the open window frame and grabs onto the cab roof to propel himself up and onto the top of the truck. Kneeling on the roof, he tosses one end of the strap over the rafter and watches it unfurl.

He grabs both ends of the strap to steady himself as he comes to a standing position on top of the truck cab. He pulls the strap several times to test that the rafter is durable. It's made of strong timber and is maybe the only support keeping the barn upright.

If he can't get the strap scooted a far enough distance from the truck cab, he knows he'll have to climb down and move the truck a foot or so. But he's able to take the ends of the two-inch-wide strap and seesaw it along the rafter. He ties a bowline knot, feeds the other end of the strap through, and pulls. After a few quick calculations, he determines the distance to be plenty sufficient.

Gabe wonders why he never before considered this method of suicide. When the guard mentioned bed sheets and hangings, it made so much sense to Gabe. And this is the perfect place. It will take days for anyone to find him. This way Willa and Evan won't have to be reminded of yet another death at The Castleton every time they look across their driveway at the utility garage.

Asphyxiation, Gabe knows, is one of the least painful ways to end one's life. Unfortunately, he doesn't know that much about hanging oneself. It seems pretty brutal. But ballooning had taught him a lot about securing a knot and that is the most important thing.

Standing on the truck roof, he completes the hangman's knot and slips the noose over his head. He faces the back of the truck and places his right foot on the top of the open driver door. He inches his right foot further out on the doorframe so that when he's ready, all he has to do is move his left foot onto the doorframe and kick the door closed beneath him.

Gabe stands balanced with his left foot on the edge of the truck cab and his right foot positioned as far out on the top of the doorframe as he can manage. He holds the noose around his neck with trembling hands. "Leesie, please, don't be mad at Daddy." He takes a deep breath—almost a gasp—and whispers, "Doing this is not about you, sweetheart. If you can hear me, you must always know your daddy loves you with all his heart. I *love* you, Leesie Anne." He lifts his chin, but tears stream down his cheeks. "Irish, you were so good. You gave me your heart every day, always. You gave me a *reason* to love. A reason to *live*. Now *all* my reasons to live are gone. What was it you said in your note, your love lives on? But I can't feel it, Irish. I can't *feel* your love. I would almost want to live if I could feel your love. I almost wish you could save me … "

A barn owl swoops past Gabe's head and perches on the truck roof. What the hell? Balanced the way he is, Gabe can only wiggle his left boot to try and shoo the owl off the truck. "Go away!" The owl dives into the truck bed and lands on the brown package. "Get outta here!" The owl claws at the wrapping paper where it's torn. "Stop that!" The owl continues clawing, its talons cutting like razors through the wrapping. Shreds of brown paper fly into the air. "That's *Leesie's* quilt!" Gabe slides his right foot back onto the truck cab. Standing with both feet on the truck roof, he lifts the noose from his neck and whips it around in the air like a lasso in an effort to scare away the owl. "Leave the quilt *alone.*" The owl screeches. Gabe holds firmly onto the noose with one hand ready to defend himself should the owl attack. "Fine. Bring it on. But you're not going to destroy that quilt. It's the *only thing* I have *left!*"

The clawing stops. The bird pivots its head to reveal a barn owl's signature heart-shaped face. Didn't Irish always say she wore her hair a certain way to complement her heart-shaped face? "*Irish?*"

Oh, God, he's hallucinating again, like this morning, thinking Irish is there, back from the dead. But. But what if the owl *is* Irish?

Irish, if it's you, please, please, let me know." The owl's haunting eyes blinked three times. Irish," Gabe whispers, "oh, Irish, please, I need you." The owl spreads its wings, Gabe can't help thinking, like an angel and rises above Gabe's head. The only sound is a gentle swoosh as it vanishes through an opening in the barn roof.

Gabe releases the noose and falls to his knees onto the metal truck roof. He curls into a fetal position. What just happened? He was one step from kicking the door closed and ending it all. But, he was outwitted by a snowy barn owl with a face in the shape of a heart and eyes nearly as unforgettable as Irish's.

Irish's eyes. He thinks back to the scene in the prison. He fought having to face Cooder Ward. He struggled with looking at the man who murdered Leesie and into eyes that had once been Irish's. But for what it's worth, Gabe kept his end of the bargain. Thankfully, as it turns out, he didn't have to live, even for a few hours, with anything other than the memories he *wanted* to hold of Irish.

He has no strength to proceed with his plan, not yet. Once he rests he can try again. He is, after all, in an abandoned barn in the middle of nowhere. Time is not an issue.

It comes to him he still needs to add to his suicide note in the van's glove box, P.S. No funeral – or memorial. Well, he'll have to let that go. That was before he changed his plan from using the van to climbing on the truck roof with a tow strap in the abandonded barn.

He closes his eyes, picturing Willa at his funeral in the black dress she wore to her daughter and granddaughter's services. Would her stoic façade crumble for him like it had for her daughter? Her granddaughter? Would Evan's voice crack when he gave Gabe's eulogy? He knew Michael would comfort his parents and Scot would comfort Michael. Jon and Sandy would hold on for dear life to each other's hands. Mr. Arnold from the hardware store might be there, and Dr. Mac would likely show his respects. Gabe had a wild thought. What if Michael talked Mr. Bergen into making an exception and letting Destiny attend the service? Destiny. The golden would continue loving unconditionally, but most likely wouldn't ever be the quite same joyful dog with all three of his close family gone. Gabe pictures Wendel Sulley, always self-conscious about grease under his fingernails, sitting in the back.

Wendel Sulley. God. How will Wendel forgive himself for selling Gabe the tow strap? Or being the last person to see Gabe alive? Wendel might think he should have known something was up. He might believe he could have stopped Gabe. Yep, Wendel might think, Gabe pulling in three times in one day, he should have known something was up. Why, Wendel might say, I even said something to Gabe about keeping the station open late, in case he needed something else. But Gabe, Wendel Sulley might say, just waved over his shoulder. I should have done something, Wendel Sulley might say until his dying breath, to stop Gabriel Hart from taking his life. Gabriel George Hart would be alive today, Wendel Sulley might say, if I'd never sold him that tow strap.

Wendel Sulley was a simple man just doing his job, trying to feed his family and greet every day with a smile. Would he be tormented *his whole life* that he hadn't asked Gabe what the heck he wanted with a dang tow strap? Tears fill Gabe's eyes.

Gabe gazes up at the yellow strap dangling from the rafter. He looks beyond it at the hole in the barn roof where the heart-faced owl had appeared and then vanished. Moments before the owl materialized, like an angel, like Irish, Gabe had wanted to *feel* her love. Could he not feel it now? Hadn't he said he wished she'd save him? *Well then?*

Every muscle in his body aches. Every bone feels like it might break. But he manages to lower himself off the truck roof and into the cab. The pain in his heart makes it impossible to turn the key in the ignition. It will be an hour before he'll use headlights to locate the deep tire ruts and make his way out of the remote cornfield.

## THIRTY-NINE

### GABE – Rest in Peace

From where Gabe sits on a porch stoop, he takes a deep breath and stands when he catches the first glimpse of Charlene Ward's red hair.

"Hello, Mrs. Ward. Hope I didn't startle you."

"Oh, hello. No, Mr. Hart. Startled isn't the word I'd use."

Charlene climbs two of the three wide porch steps and stops on the tread where Gabe stands.

"I don't think we've actually met," Gabe says, extending his hand which Charlene takes in a warm handshake, the purse on her arm swinging until she covers it with her other hand.

"Would you care to come in, Mr. Hart?"

"No, thanks. I'll only stay a minute. Irish had asked me to mail this to you over a year ago." He pulls the pink envelope addressed to Charlene from his jacket pocket. "I only just discovered it in the truck earlier today. Since it was way overdue, I decided to deliver it myself. Sorry it took so long. Looks like it's a card of some kind. She loved to send people notecards."

"Thank you for delivering this." Charlene studies the handwriting on the envelope. Under the streetlight's illumination, Gabe can see that although Charlene is close to his own age, something made her look a whole lot wiser. He thinks it might be her slightly raised eyebrows.

"Irish told me the two of you met in the cemetery parking lot one day. I know it meant a lot to her that you'd connected."

"If she were here, funny, it almost feels like she is, doesn't it, her handwriting on the envelope and all, I'm sure she'd be pleased you delivered this so that you and I could meet."

Charlene continues to study the pink envelope. A worrisome look creeps into her eyes. Gabe figures she's mentally left the porch steps. He assumes that in her mind she is in that parking lot with Irish or maybe sitting across from her husband in the visitor area of the prison.

"Mrs. Ward, I saw your husband today. I was awful. I'm sorry."

"Well, Mr. Hart, I visited him right after you left. I have to admit he was pretty shaken. But I keep asking myself how difficult it must have been for you. He, well, we, are both so sorry for … for everything." She lowers her eyes and pulls her coat collar up around her neck and buries her chin inside it.

"The temperature's dropped. I've got something else for you." Gabe wasn't expecting to but runs to the truck parked at the curb and retrieves the package from the truck bed.

"The wrapping is in rough shape; there was my dog and then this owl. Anyway, I think Irish would want you to have this."

Charlene is slow to accept the parcel. When she does, she takes a seat on the edge of the porch and cradles the bundle in her arms like it held an infant. Where the bundle was torn open, she touches the yellow butterfly fabric. "Well, I think I know what this is. Are you sure you want me ... *us* ... to have it?"

Gabe nods.

She pats the wooden porch welcoming Gabe to sit with her. "Mr. Hart, do you know how I know what this is?"

Staring at the package, Gabe shakes his head.

"Your wife would show my husband pictures of Leesie. Not right off, of course, but gradually, after she'd visited several times. And she didn't do it to make him feel bad, which I think he did at first. Your wife, I think, had a plan, and it worked. Over time, the layer of ice my husband had around his heart began to melt little by little. He stopped trying to figure out how to end his life and started looking for ways to honor your daughter's."

A wave of nausea hits Gabe. He straightens his back.

"You okay, Mr. Hart?"

He motions for her to continue.

"Well, it got so that when he talked about your daughter, there was, for lack of a better word, joy on his face and in his voice. He'd tell me about the pictures. He loved the one of your daughter in those oversized pajamas with the yellow butterflies. That was his favorite, Mr. Hart."

It is Gabe's favorite picture, too. He stands. "Better go."

Gabe's legs barely hold him as he watches cars whiz by, imagining mothers and fathers on their way home to see their kids' smiles, hear their laughter, help them with homework and maybe watch a little TV, and later, tuck them into a warm, safe bed.

"I scribbled my number on the back of the envelope, if you ever need anything," Gabe adds as he moves down a step.

"Thank you. I'll keep that in mind. Mr. Hart, I know this quilt is made with love from precious memories. Are you sure … " Charlene offers the quilt back to Gabe.

Thanks, but no, he says. He wants her to have it. And he does. Maybe one day he'd be genuinely grateful the quilt saved his life, but God only knew when that day would be. The quilt with pieces of his daughter's clothing was just too painful a reminder of what was and might have been.

He does, however, run his fingers across the downy-soft fabric that had been Leesie's pjs and whispers under his breath, "Rest in peace, my little butterfly."

Gabe's standing on the bottom step when Charlene calls, "Oh, Mr. Hart, just a minute." She reaches into her coat pocket. "I found this on the shelf at Window Four. Is it yours?"

Gabe extends his hand, and Charlene places the hot air balloon pin in his palm. He clutches the shiny green shamrock.

# FORTY

## GABE – Waiting for GABE

Destiny's front paws land on Gabe's chest, causing him to fall backwards almost knocking over the porcelain umbrella stand in Michael and Scot's entryway.

"Scot!" Michael calls from the kitchen. Gabe closes the front door intending to clarify he isn't Scot, but Michael continues. "On the phone with Mom and Dad. No news yet. Got your message Gabe wasn't at the cemetery."

Gabe roughs Destiny's ears trying to quiet his yelps as they move through the softly lit dining room and stop in the arched doorway to the kitchen. He sees Michael standing at one end of the long farmhouse table opening a wine bottle, his back to the dining room.

"I know, but listen, you two." Michael speaks passionately into his cellphone perched near the edge of the table. "Don't reach into the future. I know you're worried sick about Gabe. We *all* are. But remember, Jon *saw* him at the prison just a few hours ago. We're all just waiting for Gabe …

Hey, sorry, guys, hold on. I can't hear you … Destiny." Michael pivots to face the dining room. "What on earth —"

Michael springs forward and grabs Gabe's shoulders, knocking his phone off the table onto the floor in the process. Pulling Gabe into the kitchen, Michael hugs him to his chest. "Gabe! Oh, my God, am I glad to see you!"

Michael takes a step backward and surveys Gabe like he isn't sure but what he's seeing a ghost. Michael finally releases his brother-in-law and grabs his phone off the floor. "Gabe, want to say hey to Mom and Dad?"

A wave of lightheadedness washes over Gabe. He had no idea he's been a hot topic of discussion among everyone today. But overhearing Michael's side of the conversation with his parents, it's clear they've been concerned about him.

Still, thanks but no thanks to a long, drawn-out conversation explaining his whereabouts all day, which could easily happen with Willa. He does need, however, to at least say hey to her and Evan. They both always treated him like a son, though he's never been comfortable calling them Mom and Dad, finally stopping after Irish was no longer a reason to continue the ruse.

His reluctance has never been about them. Gabe's just never far from the memory of too many kids he knew in foster care getting adopted, then "unadopted," losing two sets of parents—their biological parents, and their adopted ones. Crazy thing was, young Gabe heard those same kids sobbing through the night and still wished he'd been chosen, wished he'd been wanted, even if he'd end up being unwanted. But that was just a naive kid craving love and willing to chance losing two sets of parents.

Adult Gabe understands it's infinitely wiser to resist offers from pretend parents. The reality is one day he will lose Willa and Evan. Michael will lose them. Scot will lose them. But, after all the loss Gabe's endured, how would he bear more pain? He's lost everyone closest to him—his mother, his dad, Leesie, and Irish; all are gone. He just can't risk losing anyone else he loves.

Gabe, poised to acknowledge Willa and Evan and then get both himself and Destiny the heck out of Dodge, sees Michael brush a tear from his cheek. Maybe it's the day he's already had, probably, or who knows why, but Michael's humble display of emotion simply overwhelms Gabe. He reaches for a chairback to steady himself. For the first time in three years his emotional fog lifts just enough and Gabe considers, really and truly, the unbearable loss Michael has suffered. And the true depth of Willa and Evan's grief. Never has he honestly, not really, given thought to how they still manage to crawl out of bed every morning and function in the world. And what about today? How did they all get through today when each feared something horrible had happened to him? They sure as hell didn't isolate. They gathered strength from one another to determine if something awful had happened, and if so, based on what he'd overhead Michael say, they knew they wouldnavigate whatever it might be together.

Over the last three years, has Gabe ever known this family to distance themselves from each other during a crisis to avoid more pain, even pain they knew was inevitable let alone unspeakable—the tragic loss of their young daughter, sister, grandchild, niece? Never. Through every heartbreak and tragedy, this family has pulled together. They've loved each other through unbearable sorrow. Unconditionally. Only one person abstained.

Gabe shakes his head. This family's been waiting for him much longer than today.

Michael steps backward, like he's reading into Gabe's head gesture that he doesn't want to speak with Willa and Evan. Gabe's first impulse is to jump at the opportunity he's been given to grab Destiny and run. But the day's unpredictable twists and turns continue, and Gabe resists the urge to bolt. Instead, like some unknown force has come over him—Irish?—he leans in and rests his palm on his brother-in-law's arm. His plan had been to simply acknowledge Willa and Evan, however, that notion flies out the window when the naïve kid in foster care surfaces after years and pulls at Gabe's heart for what may be a last chance to know how it feels to have parents. Gabe's face grows hot. Too much. Maybe, but aren't the perfect parents waiting at the other end of the line? Gabe hears a voice so low and raspy from fatigue and spent emotions that he barely recognizes it as his own. "Hey ... Mom and Dad."

Gabe releases Michael's arm and collapses against the dining room doorway. If he never again has that much attention drawn to him, he'll be grateful. Fortunately, Michael has returned to his animated self and is speaking hurriedly into the phone. "Right, guess you heard Gabe, eh? Uh, yep, he's here and Destiny is one happy pup. So, um, yeah, okay, so when do you think you can get here for dinner?"

A million thoughts race through Gabe's mind, still he appreciates how it's so like Michael to try and make an incredibly awkward situation comfortable for everyone. And how so out of character for Willa and Evan to still be at home instead of here, wolfing down Michael's famous bruschetta appetizer. And how at any minute Scot will breeze through the front door and shoo anyone in the kitchen to the living room so he can begin preparing Michael's most requested chicken schnitzel or Willa's favorite meatloaf.

Michael rolls his eyes at Gabe and makes talking-like gestures with his hand indicating he can't get his parents off the phone. When Gabe hears the front door open, he welcomes a chance to escape the kitchen and further distance himself from the phone conversation. Gabe slowly follows Destiny toward the entryway to help Scot with groceries.

Halfway through the dining room Gabe pauses. The man standing inside the front door is not Scot. Instead there stands the one person Gabe has known longer than he even knew Irish. The man Gabe is going to ask help him get the balloon working again. When they can talk about exactly how long they have been friends. And was it ninth or tenth grade they "borrowed" a car to take a spin around the block that resulted in replacing three mailboxes? The one person Gabe needs to tell how much it meant he never made fun of some kid in foster care wearing the same clothes two or three days in a row or teased him for not having parents. The man Gabe owes an apology for his insufferable behavior the last three years.

Gabe steps into the entry hall. He regrets with every fiber of his being—and likely always will—that he wasn't there for Leesie. It should have been him. It should have been her daddy.

But the man standing inside the front door was with Leesie when she … when she … Go on, Gabe. When she died. Leesie is dead. She's dead.

And if not for this man, Leesie would have died alone, without loving arms to hold her or caring words to comfort her. Mercifully, their precious Leesie, didn't die alone.

Only one person to thank for that.

"Hey, Jon."

# Epilogue

The air inside Summit Funeral Home is as musty as Gabe remembers when he enters through the side door. His knees are shaky, and his throat has a lemon-sized lump, but he's grateful to see her name spelled correctly. He's arrived several minutes late, as planned, so he can slip in unnoticed after the service has begun. He quietly takes a seat along the back wall.

The lump in his throat grows to feel the size of a cantaloupe as folks in the front of the room speak from the podium, calling the deceased by her given name.

Why did he ever think he could do this? Return to the very room where they held Leesie's funeral three years ago to the day, and one year ago for Irish's service. Attending the funeral was a grave mistake. He silently assures Irish, yes, he gets the pun. But he's still leaving.

Moving to the edge of his chair, he feels a nudge on his right shoulder. Oh, please, don't let it be anyone he knows. He ventures a glance and is surprised to see it's simply a big yellow sunflower head come to rest on the right shoulder of his jacket. The weight of its many petals and seeds apparently caused it to bow from a huge arrangement of sunflowers he'd not previously noticed. He manages to upright the bloom and brace it using a neighboring sunflower supported by a thin wire stake.

He spots a white notecard dangling precariously from the arrangement, and in tucking it back among the sunflowers, he reads the inscription. *Love you always, Leesie.* Seeing his daughter's name that way, though the sentiment was meant for Mrs. Hisey, makes his heart ache.

Now he really must leave. Thank God no one's noticed he's here, even with the sunflower incident. He slips out during a prayer and exits the building using the side door where Destiny waits curled in a warm spot of sunlight. The dog greets Gabe energetically then darts for the truck in the parking lot.

Trailing in Destiny's wake, Gabe sees out of the corner of his eye several remnant sunflower petals on his right jacket shoulder. He gently brushes them off and watches the yellow petals float to the ground. He wishes he'd thought to send flowers. Clearly someone very close to Mrs. Hisey sent the special sunflower arrangement.

Gabe opens the truck's driver door and Destiny bounds onto the seat. Midway through the ritual of instructing the dog to scootch to the passenger side, Gabe looks over his shoulder at the funeral home. Actually, aren't there are two ways to interpret the note with the special sunflowers? One obvious conclusion is the recipient of the note is Leesie Hisey. After all, it *is* her funeral. But what if "Leesie" is the sender? *Love you always, Leesie.* His Leesie?

Get real. Gabe climbs into the truck, starts the engine, and speeds out of the parking lot.

Throughout the evening, though, Gabe finds himself pacing and thinking more and more about Mrs. Hisey's funeral. Why on earth did he go? Yes, of course, he'd gone out of respect, but after hearing the name Leesie over and over, there was a moment he felt himself transported to the upstairs hall above the drug store, when he and Irish named their precious newborn baby girl after Mrs. Hisey, who thank God had been there to help bring their daughter into the world.

And what about that notecard with the name Leesie in the sunflowers? When will he shake the idea the message could have been meant for him, from his Leesie? *Love you always, Leesie.* Sure, and the giant sunflower nudged him to get his attention. He needs air.

Just shy of midnight Gabe pulls on his jacket and follows Destiny through the kitchen door and across the porch. While Destiny surveys the backyard, Gabe pauses on the porch step to study the stars above Piney Valley, half-hoping to see a meteor, like he had a few days before. Funny, it's been forever since he's thought about the evening he and Leesie sat on the back porch step discussing meteors and angels. Glancing over his shoulder, he half-hopes to see Irish standing there, the way she'd observed the two of them from the kitchen doorway that night.

Irish. Oh, Irish, a whole lot of half-hoping going on tonight. "But Irish, I kept my promise to you," he whispers into the night.

Actually breaking his promise to Irish was never an option because he knew that would have come at an untold price. Still, Gabe never expected that doing the right thing, keeping his promise, would also come at a price. He's unsure if it happened in the barn when he pleaded with Leesie to forgive her daddy or maybe at the prison when Jon shared her final words. He wishes he could pinpoint the moment so maybe he could fix it. But he has no idea. All he knows is, since three days ago, he no longer feels any emotional connection with Leesie. Oh, of course he still loves her, now more than *ever*. But the love has nowhere to go, like it's disappearing into a black hole. He looks up at the sky. "Yes, Irish, I'm finally ready for a sign."

From the moment he lost Leesie until three days ago, his emotional connection with his little girl had presented as immobilizing remorse and regret, but at least it was *something*.

He doesn't know but what his quest to rekindle a bond with Leesie led him earlier in the day to Mrs. Hisey's funeral. Sitting in the same room of his little girl's funeral and hearing the name Leesie spoken aloud did cause him to feel *something*. Even if he isn't able to describe what that something was … is … was.

And maybe Irish rubbed off on him more than he likes to admit, but he's still obsessed with that notecard. Why couldn't it be *from* Leesie, not to Lessie? And who's to say the giant yellow sunflower *didn't* deliberately land on his shoulder? A crazy notion, to be sure, but they both made him feel the visceral connection he longs to have again with his sweet little girl.

Beyond a crazy notion, and why he avoids feelings.

Destiny ignores Gabe's call to go inside the house. The dog clearly has unfinished business in the shrubs along the utility garage. Gabe takes a seat on the top porch step to wait it out and shoves his bare hands deep inside his jacket pockets for warmth.

Immediately Gabe stands and turns as though propelled by some unearthly force to enter the house, removing only his left hand from a pocket to navigate the door. Destiny, unsummoned, appears close at Gabe's heels.

One day Gabe may look back and remember the moment differently, but he's drawn to the dim light above the kitchen sink much as he was a few days before when he wrote the suicide note, when he'd thought all hope was gone.

There at the kitchen counter, in the dim light, Gabe stands with Destiny's warm head pressed against him, his nose nudging his right jacket pocket. Does Dest have an idea of what amazing discovery is cradled in Gabe's palm?

Perhaps if Gabe didn't want so much for it to be a sign from Leesie, he would make an excuse for what he has found in his pocket. But it's been a long day, a long year, a long three years, and he welcomes the tears streaming from his eyes, and the possibilities his open palm reveals, as he gently places on the kitchen counter the child-size handful of yellow sunflower petals.

# *Waiting for Gabe* by Diana Black
# Book Club Questions

The following questions are offered as opportunities to further explore *Waiting for Gabe*.

1. How did Gabe's childhood in foster care inform his decisions as an adult?
2. Would you ever be able to forgive Cooder Ward? Why or why not? What if he hadn't left the scene of the accident?
3. Did you find Irish to be a believable character? Why or why not? More so when she was dead or alive? How did you feel about Irish's vet visit scheme?
4. In what significant ways did Irish's grief manifest? How did you feel about the quilt?
5. Did you feel Irish's family's affection for Gabe influence him? Willa? Evan? Michael?
6. Was it believable Jon Elam would berate Cooder Ward during the medical exam?
7. Can you understand Gabe being angry at Jon for being with Leesie when she died?
8. How did Leesie, Gabe and Cooder's childhoods differ? How were they similar?
9. How did Mrs. Hisey character move the story? Was it satisfying? Why or why not?
10. How did you feel during the prison scene when Gabe visits Cooder? Did you sympathize with his behavior toward Cooder? Jon? Why or why not?

11. Does it matter Cooder was no longer sitting across from Gabe when he finally managed to look through the glass? Had Gabe honored his promise to Irish?
12. How significant was it that Gabe chose the abandoned barn over taking his life at home?
13. Were you surprised Gabe gave the memory quilt to Cooder's wife? Why or why not?
14. Was the epilogue necessary? Why or why not?
15. Did you feel Gabe underwent a realistic character arc? Why or why not?
16. Did Cooder undergo a satisfying character arc? Why or why not? Was Irish's relationship with him believable? Why or why not?
17. Were there any quotes or passages that stood out to you? Did humor help lighten the serious theme and nature of the book?
18. Did the title live up to the storyline? Why or why not?
19. Was the book satisfying to read? Why or why not? Would you recommend it?
20. What burning question do you still have about the book, plot, or characters?

# Acknowledgements

*"My great hope is to laugh as much as I cry; to get my work done and try to love somebody and have the courage to accept the love in return."*
—*Maya Angelou*

To Michael, my better angel. To Ricky. To Mother and Dad, and Grandmother Lord. To Sandy and Tom Walts, and their fab family. To Mary and Ken Cunningham, Carol Proffitt, Wendy Pomerantz, Donna Michael, Sherry Musselwhite, and Joyce Trammell. To Team Orange, Scott Patrick, and my extended Florida fam. To Naomi Tutu and Margaret Elam. To Alive Hospice, Carrie Cox and Mary "Red Pen" Mackinnon. To my first editor, Matthew Sharpe, who never gave up on the author's arc. To Echo Montgomery Garrett and Lucid House Publishing for believing in the story, its characters and message.

# About the Author

**Diana Black** is a published nonfiction and children's author, cartoonist, and songwriter, who is excited to share with readers her first novel, *Waiting for Gabe*. The author drew inspiration for her characters and storyline in part from working with an acclaimed nonprofit hospice and co-founding The Orange Duffel Bag Initiative (ODBI), an award-winning public charity supporting students experiencing foster care or homelessness.

Diana's lifelong fascination with three universal literary themes—death, forgiveness, and family—motivates her characters in *Waiting for Gabe*. While her novel delves deeply into matters of life-and-death, the author's love of humor and its life-affirming qualities create magical moments that provide a distinct perspective on the human experience. Strength of female characters in her work of fiction celebrates women who in real life forever influenced the writer—her maternal grandmother, who exemplified kindness and independence, and her English lit teacher, whose steadfast belief in a teenager changed the trajectory of her life.

Diana has devoted the last 12 years to her nonprofit, affectionately referred to as Team Orange, where on any given day she may be found writing a grant in the morning followed by presenting in the afternoon at a national conference focused on youth experiencing homelessness or foster care to answering a text during dinner to assist an ODBI program alum in need. In her precious spare hours, she treasures time with her daughter and granddaughter, family and friends, and enjoys reading, golf, tennis, and long beach walks on the Florida barrier island she calls home.

To learn more about Diana's work as vice president of the nonprofit Orange Duffel Bag Initiative and young people aging out of foster care, please visit www.theODBI.org

Printed in the USA
CPSIA information can be obtained
at www.ICGtesting.com
LVHW010424110924
790678LV00003B/4

9 781950 495566